Satiate

M.A. Cobb

Preface

This book contains incredibly dark themes.
For a complete list visit www.macobb.com

Don't say I didn't warn you...

This book is best read with a ginger ale tonic
a package of crackers
and a comfort plushy.

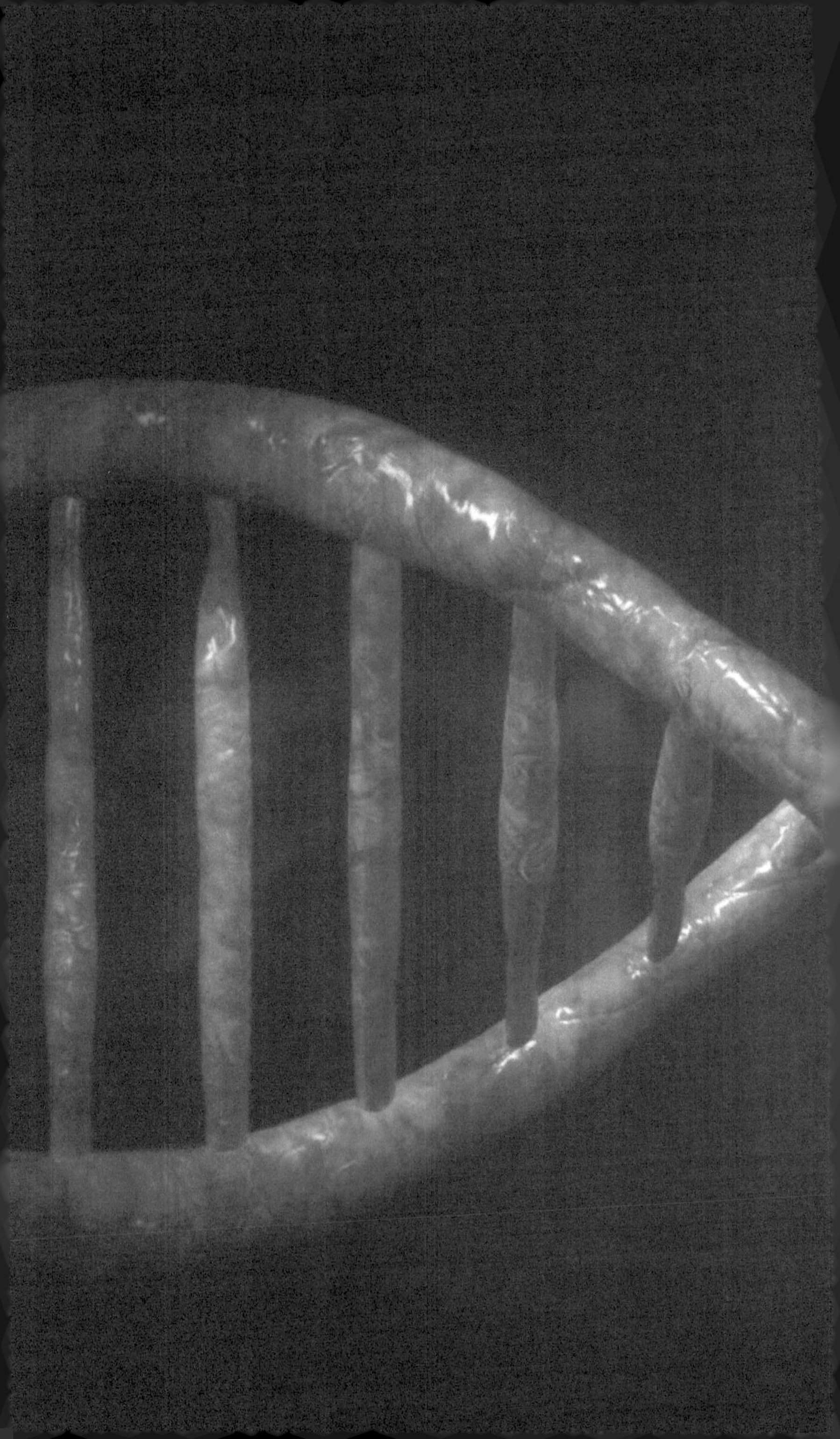

Chapter 1

Caleb

"Wait. What?" My knuckles turn white as I squeeze the edge of the stainless steel workbench. "Please, repeat what you just said."

"The delivery virus wasn't thoroughly scrubbed before it was used." The gangly tech shifts his weight and avoids meeting my stare.

I take an arduous breath as I struggle to keep myself from screaming, or beating him.

"Which batch? If it's the most recent one, we can do a recall. There's a good chance they aren't in circulation." Going down the mental list of which hospitals are involved in the testing phase, I think there's only two that may use them more quickly.

"Um. Genevieve said it was at least the last six." He takes a faltering step away from me.

It's almost like he knows I'm tempted to wrap my hands around his throat.

Six.

We're fucked.

There are eighty four facilities just in the United States using our new medication. Another fifty overseas.

Raw rage blurs my vision as the table in front of me flies with a boost from my foot. My voice cracks from the force of my roar. "No!" I grab the front of his white clinical jacket. "Do you have any idea what this means?"

His large blue eyes grow shiny with tears that soak into the top of the mask covering his nose. "No, sir."

The heat of his exhale reeks of onions as it wafts into my face.

"It means—" I push him to arm's length. "—that we've released an appetite inducer designed for cancer patients with accelerated healing properties."

His red eyebrows knot over his nose. "But, sir? Is that bad?"

I can't even look at him. How can he be this stupid?

Freeing my hands from his lapels, I rub them into my eyes until I see starbursts.

"No, that part was doing great. Working beautifully, even. The absolute shit part is we also just infected them with a purified and enhanced form of rabies." Collapsing back into my chair, I wish the table was still sitting there so I could rest my elbows on it.

My phone vibrates in my pocket.

Carmen.

Dammit.

"I have to go. Clean up this mess. Then call your mom. Tell her you love her. Find a hole and crawl in it." Striding past him, I find myself rushing down the sterile hall.

Her name is embossed on a brushed brass plaque. Too bad that fancy plate won't save us.

"Caleb. I see we are past the knocking stage?" Her large brown eyes narrow when I burst in.

"I quit." Waiting for a reaction, I'm a little disappointed when she smiles.

"It won't be that bad. I understand that there was an oversight in the quality control?" Her thin fingers sort a stack of papers on her desk as she watches me.

"Oversight? That's the understatement of the year. Let's just hope the patients are all bed ridden invalids. I *told* you not to use that subcontractor for scrubbing the vectors." I've seen the effects of rabies on a human during my Phd studies. That was the wild version, not the lab perfected, ultra-refined, steroid version we use as a gene therapy delivery system.

"I very much doubt that will be necessary. I've talked to the director of the CDC, he assured me that they are keeping a very close eye out for adverse reaction reports."

My stomach rolls. If the government is already involved, there's been issues.

"Can we at least get the word out? Set up a vaccine schedule so people can protect themselves?" The vibrating notifications in my pocket are getting more frequent. My colleagues are catching wind of this.

"That was brought to the board, but declined. Without further proof of a complication, it's being left to the medical institutions to take care of things." Her lipstick leaves a smear as she takes a sip from a white mug.

We send out a new batch every three days.

Eighteen days since the first rounds were sent.

I bet most of those sat in a cooler for at least the first week. So we have either three days, or ten before all hell breaks loose.

Her red nails glare in contrast to her black hair when she sweeps it away from her face. "Take today off. Tomorrow, I need you back here so you can run some extrapolation data on possible adverse effects."

"Oh, that part is easy. We're on the one way track to crazy town." I pull the door nearly shut as I step into the cool hall.

Wait. I almost forgot.

I push my head back through the door. "I really quit."

The little spiderweb of red lines radiate around my brown irises in the mirror. I haven't really slept in four days, and it's starting to really show. My body and my apartment are both worse for wear. All I can do is doom scroll on my phone and manically re-search every strange occurrence that happens near the hospitals on our delivery schedule.

Ours. I mean theirs. I had this gnawing feeling that something would break loose and I'm glad to not be tied to that company anymore.

What the fuck do I do now?

I feel like I'm stuck in limbo. I *know* shit is going to go down, I just don't know when. Or, how badly.

Carmen has texted me every morning to ask if I was coming in. Maybe if she's still asking next month I'll go back.

Yesterday's coffee sits with an oily ring in the pot. I'm tempted to pour some bourbon in and take a real nap.

The buzzing of my cell makes me jump. I really need to sleep, I'm getting frazzled.

"Hey, Steve. I'm still not coming back." He's the closest thing I have to a friend at the lab. As the official 'rat guy', I don't think he has a lot of people that talk to him.

"Not this time. Today's my last day, too." His voice is a heavy whisper. It sounds quite a bit different from his normal nasally tone.

"Why? Did something happen?" I lean against my air conditioner. The summer heat is already kicking up.

"They shut us down." There's a thumping sound and muffled voices in the background.

"Who? What's going on?" The sun streaming through the window is more appealing as a cold shiver runs up my spine.

"The CDC. They're taking everything. I have to go. Stay safe, Caleb."

There's a little thrill knowing I was right. Until it morphs into gripping nausea that has me running to the bathroom. Dispelling the morning's coffee doesn't make me feel any better.

If they're already buttoning up loose ends, that means that something big is already started.

The lure of the liquor pulls me back into my small living room.

A shriek echoes from outside.

What the hell?

The big picture window of my second floor apartment overlooks a big parking lot. Two boys, around ten years old, scream and jump through a sprinkler at one end of the asphalt.

Funny, they look a lot like my best friend and I when we were kids.

Hmm. I haven't talked to Levi in a few days. His family has a big cabin a few miles outside of town. It might be time to talk him into a long visit up there, away from the crowds.

He made me promise when I chose to study viruses that if there was ever an impending threat to let him know.

This old backpack should work perfectly. I start grabbing clothes and food to toss in as I hit the call button.

"Caleb! Hey, how's it going? Calling on a weekday?" He always sounds happy. Even when I broke his hand when we were fourteen. He laughed the whole time they were setting it.

"Hi, buddy. Remember that promise I made you?"

Chapter 2

Jessica

"There is no way you're making me stay in a filthy cabin, Levi." I cross my arms and push up my breasts in a hope that I can distract him from this ridiculous notion.

"Jess, we have to. Caleb called and said shit is going to hit the fan." He stuffs something rolled into a hiking bag that's covered in cobwebs from the garage.

Hideous.

"Fine. You go. I've got plans this weekend to meet my friends at Viva la Vida. So, while you're playing in the dirt, I'll be drinking daiquiris." The best money I've ever spent is at the hairdresser's to give me the perfect twirl of my blonde curly hair as I flip around and walk away from him.

Let him watch my ass in these heels and still decide to go.

"You're going, Jessica." His tone is gruff. Final.

My hands fly to my hips defiantly as I pivot on one of my four inch stilettos. "No, Levi. I'm not going where there are bugs and sticks. That's caveman shit. I don't know what your friend told you, but nothing is going to happen."

He moves so fast, I don't even register it until his hands are wrapped around my wrists and his head drops so his blue eyes hover inches from mine. "Do you know what Caleb does? He works with viruses. Very dangerous ones. If he says I need to get out of town for a while, I'm not questioning him."

I hate this so much.

"How long?" My lower lip juts on its own, so I push it out into an exaggerated pout.

"He said by the end of a month we'd have a better idea of how things are going down." His long fingers unwrap from my arms. "Go pack. Plan ahead. There's no delivery or take out. Whatever you bring had better last you at least a month, because once we get to the cabin, we aren't leaving." He points in the direction of our room. "And you better pick some realistic clothes. That dress will be hard to chop wood in." A lopsided grin pulls at his lips before he turns away.

My shoe clicks on the marble as I stomp my foot. "Are you fucking serious? I am not a lumberjack!" But why does my mind go to that cute flannel shirt I bought last fall? And I have a clunky leather boot that would look fabulous with it.

Maybe this won't be so bad. It will give me the chance to build a few more followers.

"First time for everything, Jess. Now, go." Levi turns away to pick up his medical bag and backpack before disappearing through the door that leads to the garage.

At least this will give me the chance to use the adorable pink couture luggage I bought in hopes of a trip to France this fall.

This little excursion into primitive life had better be over by then.

***

My worst nightmare.

It's small. At best three thousand square feet. Almost a hovel. Trees everywhere. A pond? Gross. It has green on the surface and everywhere I look there are bugs.

Levi hasn't even put our Land Rover in park and I'm already wishing we could leave.

"How long do we have to stay here?" I don't want to open the door. The musty smell of *earth* is already infiltrating the interior and overpowering the leather.

My stomach rolls as my new reality sets in.

The back hatch opens and he grabs the first two of my bags. "I told you. At least a month. Now, come and help carry shit in." His temper has been getting shorter with every mile passed.

Like this is my fault. He should have just let me stay home.

The humidity hits first, then the buzzing of insects. This is hell.

My matching makeup case sits near the edge, so I dutifully pick it up to carry.

"Jesus, Jess. Is that all you're going to get? One tiny ass bag?" Each of his arms are full of groceries we picked up along the way.

"What do you expect of me, Levi?" I can hear the shrillness of my own voice, but I don't care. "The wheels on my luggage won't work in *mud!*" My hair is already flattened from the drive, but it still whips marvelously around my shoulders. I'm going to absolutely die without being able to see my stylist for a month. A brown paper sack covering my head will be an improvement over my roots growing out.

Wet clay sticks to the bottom of my designer boots. The rain we drove through must have hit here this morning.

Trudging through the sticky mess, it's a relief when I finally step onto the wooden stairs leading to a large wrap around porch. Like the kind you see in one of those awful rural design magazines. Give me modern any day. Even industrial would be better than this travesty.

My god. There's even a hillbilly rocking chair.

"You're going to love this, Jess. It will be a nice break from Malibu." Levi throws a flashy white smile over his shoulder before pushing open the wooden door.

"Nobody wants a break from Malibu, Levi. Only crazy people want to live in the woods." This house stinks. Like musty mothballs. How do humans live like this? I'm afraid to sit on the sheet draped furniture. It might infect me with its peasant-ness.

"You're so damned dramatic. It's almost like your father isn't a plumber. What happened to the free spirited girl I married?" He pulls a drape from the kitchen counter, revealing a burnt yellow colored formica top.

I think I just puked a little in my mouth. "My father *owns* a large plumbing company. He doesn't actually do any of it. You're acting like you aren't a doctor used to driving your Bentley and wearing Prada. That free spirit crap was so I could find someone wealthy enough to take care of me." I didn't find out until after we were engaged that he came from this. Nothing. He is self made. I thought he was old money. Now, I may be regretting my decision since he is obviously trying to get back in touch with his roots.

His dust encrusted ones.

Coughing my way out of the suffocating house, I stumble my way back to the porch in time to see a bright yellow Jeep pull in next to our car.

"Levi? There's someone here." A tall man with dark hair and broad shoulders unfolds himself from the newly arrived vehicle. He throws his hand up in a small wave before walking around to the rear and pulling out bags of his own.

Maybe he'll help carry my things in, too. Into this disgusting house. With both of them cleaning, it will be slightly more presentable.

But, it will take fire to make the kitchen look better.

"Caleb! How was the drive from Nevada?" Levi steps down into the overgrown yard to approach the man.

So he's the reason we're here. I don't really care how good looking he is. It's his fault.

"Good. Glad to be out of there. I'm happy you're here. How'd the missus take the news?" Caleb turns his dark eyes towards me before shaking hands with my husband.

Levi doesn't even glance at me. "She'll be fine. It'll do her some good."

He infuriates me. At least he gave up trying to drag me along with him to his functions. I wish he'd find a fucktoy like the rest of the guys his age and leave me alone.

It'd be her here and not me. Nothing would make me happier.

"Did you call her?" Caleb steps to the side, letting Levi lead the way into the house.

"Yeah, she said she'd be on her way." My husband called another woman after all? Is he having an affair?

"What the hell? You're bringing some side chick here? I knew it! Are you cheating on me and bringing your tramp into my house?" The hollow floor of the porch gives a satisfying sound when I stomp my foot in these heavy boots.

I catch the tail end of Levi rolling his eyes. It pisses me off even more.

"Chill before I spank the shit out of you in front of my friend." Levi's eyes darken in a scowl as he throws one of my bags on the floor. His sandy hair spikes when he runs his fingers through it. "He's asking about Sarah."

There's a scuff on my new pink garment bag. I can't even think. Anger boils up until I scream. "Who is Sarah?"

"I swear, Jessica. Get out of your head for a minute. It's my sister. You know that." He shakes his head as he cuts down a hallway and disappears into the back of the house.

Caleb blinks at me. "Nice to meet you." He turns and takes the stairs leading up two at a time.

Chapter 3

Sarah

"No, I won't be back next week, I'll be on vacation for one month. How many of you know how long a month is?" Just a few more hours and this school week is done. "Yes, Stacy? How long is a month?"

Her front teeth are bigger than the rest, accentuated by the missing one just to the side. "Um, a month is shorter than a year." Her large brown eyes look at me as she brightly smiles.

"Yes. You are correct. What is a month longer than?" Perhaps with the process of elimination this will go faster.

A small boy to her left timidly raises his hand. His feet swing in his seat a few inches from the floor.

"Daniel, what is a month longer than?" I can feel my fingers curling into my desk edge as I feign patience while watching him chew on his lip.

"A snake!" he cries after a moment of thinking.

Three hours and fifteen minutes. It's always when I have other plans the days slow down. I'm not sure why Levi insisted I make it up to the cabin, claiming that it was an emergency. I just hope like hell it isn't because he's having a kid with Jessica.

A shiver runs up my spine as I plaster my fake smile on while the classroom erupts into giggles.

"A month *is* longer than a snake. It's also longer than a *week*." Glancing at the clock more often doesn't make it move any faster. "What do we do on Fridays for special class?"

This curries many more rapidly waving hands.

"Oh! Oh! Miss Hart! I know!" Emily frantically waves her hand from the far side of the room.

She rarely gets excited. Except about this.

"Yes, Emily?" I do my best to give a genuine smile of encouragement.

"The library!" She gives such a melodramatic elated sigh afterwards it almost makes me giggle.

"Very good! So after four more trips to the library, I'll be back from vacation!" I hope. Levi had said when he called on Monday that I needed to pack for an extended time. He has his ear to the ground with all of his doctor buddies in L.A., he'd have a head's up if there was some sort of upheaval.

Maybe there's going to be some sort of earthquake? I've always heard a big one could devastate California.

Crap. All these kids. Should I tell them? What good would it do? I'm not even sure why I'm leaving.

"Go ahead and push in your chairs, let's line up to go to recess."

My boss tried to keep me from leaving. She mentioned that they've had an extraordinary number of teachers calling in sick this week. I've learned in the four years I've been doing this, it always seems to happen the last few weeks of school. We get burnt out as the days get longer since the kids are more restless.

I'm not exactly upset about needing to go. First grade kids can feel the calling of the sun like it's a thrum in the air, driving their little legs to jitter and their mouths often follow.

One stop to make on the way home, then I'll grab my stuff and be off to the mountains.

I'm almost home when I notice flashing lights near my house. What the hell? Is that cops and an ambulance?

Holy shit.

This is a boring neighborhood. I made sure when I bought here using my inheritance.

Maybe Levi had the better idea using his money to go to medical school.

They're at the house right next to mine? Those are the quiet neighbors. Beatrice and Brian Donaldson are in their sixties. She's in cancer treatment for crying out loud.

I hope there wasn't a robbery.

An armed officer is standing in the street, blocking my driveway.

"Can I help you, ma'am?" His hat is pulled low over his eyes, but it feels like he's scrutinizing me.

"I live right there."

He follows my pointing finger and holds out his hand. "Identification."

Please don't be expired.

With a nervous tremor, I hand him the small plastic card and wait as he reads it.

"Is everything okay? Was there a robbery?"

He hands back my driver's license and shakes his head. "Domestic issue. You'll be safe in your home." The bullet proof vest outline beneath his uniform becomes clear as he steps away and gestures for me to pass.

Whew.

Wait, what does that mean?

Should I load my car and leave right away, or hold off until they leave?

Once I'm safely in the shadow of my garage, I dig out my cell to call the person who lives just past the Donaldson's. She knows everything that goes on around here.

"Kelly? I'm sorry to bother you, but do you know what happened at Beatrice and Brian's?" I don't even bother with pleasantries. They're sweet and genuine people who always greet me with a smile and even have me over regularly for dinner.

"Sarah! Oh my god! I heard the most awful screaming and went to check! I thought someone was dying. Beatrice was on top of Brian and she was *eating* him!" Kelly has always been the local gossip and a bit of a drama queen, but the loud wailing sobs she breaks down into don't sound like she's exaggerating.

"What? That doesn't make any sense!" Beatrice weighs all of eighty pounds since she's been in chemo. Not to mention she makes the best apple pie I've ever had.

"Listen to me! She was on top of him, her face was covered in blood! She had his, his—" The line gets muffled and I hear the sounds of gagging.

Jesus. It makes my own stomach roll hearing her dry retching.

"—hanging from her mouth!" She sniffles like one of my kids trying to pull a string of snot off of their lip.

"So, Brian. Is he, um?" I don't even know if I can ask.

"He wouldn't stop squealing. It reminded me of living on the farm when we slaughtered the pigs." Her voice drops to almost a whisper. "It was the worst thing I've ever heard."

A trip out to the cabin is sounding better and better. Poor Brian. He was always so kind. His favorite thing was running the barbeque for block parties.

I'll never think of pulled pork quite the same way again.

"You know, it took six grown men to haul her away. She was fighting the whole time. I think she even bit a couple of them! What do you think would make her so crazy? Was it the cancer?" Kelly's fading whine gives me the impression she's been asking these same questions repetitively.

"I've never heard of it causing that kind of issue. You'd think she was too weak to do much? Last time I saw her, she could barely get out of bed. I'm sorry, Kelly. That must have been terrifying. I'm sure you need to rest after that. Thank you for telling me." I've made it into my house and thrown my purse on the counter, but I need to concentrate on getting the hell out of town for a while.

She breaks down and loses her voice in a hiccup riddled sob. "Yes, good night."

My mind is spinning. I'm glad I took most of this week to make lists and pack. Right now, I have no idea what direction to go. Except to the freezer for a pint of peanut butter ice cream.

A little bit of brain freeze and a lot of sweat later, I have my Subaru packed and the refrigerator cleaned out.

The last thing I want is to come back in a few weeks to rotten food.

It's almost a four hour drive before I turn onto the dirt road leading to my family's cabin.

Who's Jeep? I know Jessica didn't drive. She might chip a nail.

Being stuck here with her is going to be hell enough. Why did my brother decide to bring someone else?

A knot of nervousness forms in my belly as I catch a glance of myself in the mirror. Besides bags under my green eyes and loose strands of dark hair from my ponytail, I guess I don't look too worse for wear.

Yea, right. I look like crap. I cried half the way here thinking about poor Brian and Beatrice.

Whatever. The mystery guest will just have to deal with it. I'm not here to impress anyone.

I just hope it isn't one of Jessica's vapid friends.

My foot is just resting on the first step leading up to the porch when the front door flies open and Levi rushes out.

"You made it!" His smile is ultra bright against his tanned face. Wrapping me in a big hug helps to lift some of the weight from my soul.

We've always been those weird siblings that got along. Growing up, he's been my best friend. It's only in the last two years that we've drifted apart.

I blame *her*.

Speak of the devil. Blonde curls and ten foot long eyelashes that are only rivaled by the length of her nails. She doesn't even come to greet me, she's laid back on the couch in an odd pose holding her phone making duck faces.

"Who else is here?" I try to keep my voice low. If I don't spook Jessica, she won't focus her bitchy towards me.

He pulls back, but his hands have a firm grip on my upper arms.

That usually means he's breaking bad news.

"Well. Um. He's the reason we're here. Something bad is going to go down." One of his hands works its way through his stiff short hair as he looks over my head.

"What do you mean by 'bad'?" If I stare hard enough at him, I might be able to pick up some clue in his expression.

Poker faced bastard.

"End of the world shit, Sarah. Seriously." He's never been one for theatrics, but I wonder if it's a side effect from hanging out with all of the celebrities in Hollywood.

"Levi, you swore on our parent's graves that this was important. Now you're touting tin foil hat." He's starting to piss me off. "Who?"

"You sound like an owl." A deep voice from behind me smothers me in a flood of memories.

I don't want to turn around. My eyes are sore from crying, but new tears sting my lids.

"No. You didn't?" Clutching Levi's arms, I refuse to let go. I don't want to accept that *he's* here. If I never look, he won't be real.

My traitorous brother rips that choice from me by turning me against my will to face the person I swore I'd hate until my dying breath.

Caleb.

Chapter 4

Peter

Good behavior only goes so far. When that old fucker went nutso in the mess hall, everyone lost favor in Cell Block B. All it takes is one bad day to set back my last year and half of a flawless record.

I'm shanking that son of a bitch when I get out of the infirmary. If he isn't dead yet.

Who gives a shit that he has cancer. We all have our boo hoo stories. No one ends up in prison that had a good life.

The sins of the father tainted at least half of us. Well, the ones who admit it.

My fingers trace the scars on my arm out of habit as the medic wraps my wrist.

I still can't believe Jimmy bit me like a bitch when I wouldn't give up my food. And then had the balls to attack Denny and Flow when they tried to peel him off my arm.

He was snapping his teeth like the rabid dog that left my scars.

Those are memories I'd rather not revisit.

"He's not diseased, is he?" Can cancer spread like herpes? I don't want to undergo the rounds of shots I had to suffer after that pit bull attack. I hate needles. Half the nasty asses in here have some sort of std. I'd rather not.

All the women I've been with were virgins. I killed the whores.

They aren't much good once they've been used.

"No, Pete. He had to get tested regularly. You'll be fine." The lack of empathy from the bland faced tech makes me want to punch him in the throat just to see his expression change.

I'm already on thin ice after the riot at lunch. There's a pretty good chance I'll be pissing blood for a week after the baton bashing my kidneys took to break up the fight. My knuckles are already split open and bleeding.

Squinting at the razor burn on his oversized Adam's apple, I'm too busy weighing the pros and cons of pressing my fist against it at a high velocity to notice he's finished and pulling his gloves off.

Five of the seven beds are filled with inmates being treated, guards ringing us like seagulls lurking over a french fry. They're just waiting to beat us again. I can see the lust and rage in their faces.

I've seen it in my own blue eyes in the mirror. The need for violence that makes my cock stand up and my fingers grip the air until they find a neck to squeeze.

My knee bounces. I need to get out of here and back to my bed so I can jerk this tension into the mattress.

"Hands out." One of the young officers steps forward dangling a pair of cuffs from his finger. The fresh ones like him always have a chip on their shoulder. He doesn't know how thin the skin is over that pulsing artery running along his throat, or how little pressure it actually takes to make the blood stop flowing.

He'd be nicer if he did.

The cuffs make my wrist itch under the gauze.

By the time they've escorted me back to my bed, the feeling of ants crawling over me has spread up my arm and across my chest.

"I need to go back. There's something wrong." Fire is erupting in my pits and beneath my jaw. A cold sweat prickles along my hair.

"Don't be such a pussy, Pete. You only got a scratch." Peach fuzz slides my door until it clicks and then pulls his key to take off the manacles on my wrists. "Next time, just give Jimmy the snack. He looks like he needs it."

"Like hell I will." Turning away from the bars, my stomach rolls as I stumble to my bed. No longer flooded with rage, my body is a frigid volcano of shivers and heat.

Red lines work their way up my arm and I curl into a ball against the concrete wall. Screams echo through the halls before I close my eyes.

Are they coming from me?

Voices melt their way out of the darkness. Beeping and metal clanging barrage me until a loud bang startles me to look around.

Where the fuck am I?

Curtains hang around my bed, but it's a gurney. My right wrist is tethered to a rail.

When did I get to the hospital? Shit, I must have really blacked out.

There's rapid footsteps and garbled voices, but none of it is clear.

"Hello?" I sound like I had a three day bender and puked the last third.

The blue wall shrieks back on stiff casters, thrown apart by a petite woman in pink scrubs. But, damn, she's hot with that little brunette ponytail.

"Hiya, blondie. Glad to see you're awake. I'll have your nurse come in for you." She flashes me a tight smile before jerking the curtain back into place.

She's the first chick I've seen outside of a magazine in a year. My cock raises to attention, a stiff reminder of just how long it's been since I've been able to sink into one.

My bandaged hand reflexively moves to cover the tenting fabric over my crotch.

Huh. That didn't hurt the wound on my wrist. It sure as hell did when Jimmy bit me and it was throbbing when I laid down.

Using my teeth and my bound hand as well as I can, I rip through the layers of wraps to find my skin is whole and smooth.

How long have I been out? Jimmy's teeth had laid back the fleshy part above my thumb. I could see my fucking tendons when I managed to pummel him enough to free myself.

Not a mark. Or a scar?

Rapid movement and yelling erupts from some place down a hall. Maybe they're in the next room, but it's muffled.

A crash echoes over me followed by a heavy thump.

Jesus. Sounds like a fight.

I can't. That's my rap that got me put away. They don't know about any of my other shit and I want to keep it that way.

Even after the scrap in the cafeteria, I'm still slated to be released in only three more months.

The sweet little ass on that girl that checked on me might be worth an extra stay if I get the chance.

Groaning distracts me. I think it's coming from just a few feet away from me.

A weird click punctuates the end of each moan.

Twisting on the wobbly gurney, I can barely reach the blue checkered curtain to brush it back.

It's just a kid. Well, teen. He's curled in a ball with his hands fixed with velcro straps to the sides.

"You alright, buddy?"

Why do they have him tied down? Is he a convict?

His head snaps to face me when I speak. Jerking hard enough to almost tip his stretcher, his fingers reach like claws in my direction and his teeth snap.

That's the clicking I heard.

Just like Jimmy.

Something coils in my guts sending acid burning through my limbs. This must be what fear feels like.

I need to get away from him. The wild look on his face and the tearing at the air as he strains against his restraints show his dedication to his attempt to reach me.

That dude will kill me if he gets loose.

Shuffling and more loud voices converge away from us. There's a big tussle going on and I want to be the opposite way of all of this crazy.

No one is here. The guard that is supposed to be watching me is missing. I bet he's involved in whatever huge throw down is going on.

A loud pop throws my neighbor into overdrive. He bucks his hips hard enough that he tips his bed over with a crash.

"You just stay on your side, hombre. No need to be all chompy." Scrambling to get away from him, I'm limited by the cuff holding my wrist.

It isn't tight. Luck might be on my side.

This is going to hurt.

The first hard tug gets the sharp metal bracelet to the tip of my thumb knuckle, but it digs in like a bastard, cutting into the skin.

Thin fingers spasm over the edge of my bedside.

Fuck. He's free.

"No, no, no you don't!" Another hard yank. Holy shit that peeled the flesh back like a banana peel. Blood pours over my wrist and palm.

Dammit. So close.

Red stars burst on the corners of my vision as I pull as hard as I can. It feels like my thumb is being torn from my body as the tendons stretch and rip, dislocating it to lay flat.

I did it.

Gritting my jaw to keep from yelling out, I manage to slip off the side of the bed just as the second hand reaches up to grab the rails.

He pulls himself up and leaps at me.

An IV pole makes a handy obstacle to push him back, but my mangled thumb makes it hard to hold.

"Don't do that again." The metal rod has a seam in the center, so I rip the top half off and wield it like a sword.

"Hungry." His voice doesn't fit his body. It's deep, primal, more of a growl than language. His gown wraps around his skinny frame flashing a pair of whitey tighties hanging off his hips.

Pointing the end of the stand at him should keep him at bay.

Or not.

With a feral scream, he jumps at me.

And impales himself through the neck on my makeshift weapon. He still tries to reach out at me with the rod sticking right in the center of his throat. Blood sprays behind him making a purple arc on the blue curtain.

Gurgling, he pushes another step closer and rams the tube deeper until it appears behind his head.

Freak. I gotta get that out of him and stab him again.

And again.

And twice more. Crimson paints the room and drips from my face, but the psycho kid finally stops moving with one last snap of his teeth.

Now, I'm really screwed.

I can't let anyone see this or I'll go to prison for the long haul.

Not going to happen.

Ripping off my own hospital garb, I run in the opposite direction from where I hear all the noise coming. In nothing but a pair of prison boxers, I am running as fast as my bare feet can carry me.

A big metal door with a push bar is lit up like a Vegas strip club and it's calling to me in neon exit letters.

It doesn't stand a chance and flies open with my full weight thrown against it.

The void of night lurks just past the low whine of a halogen glow.

I'm free.

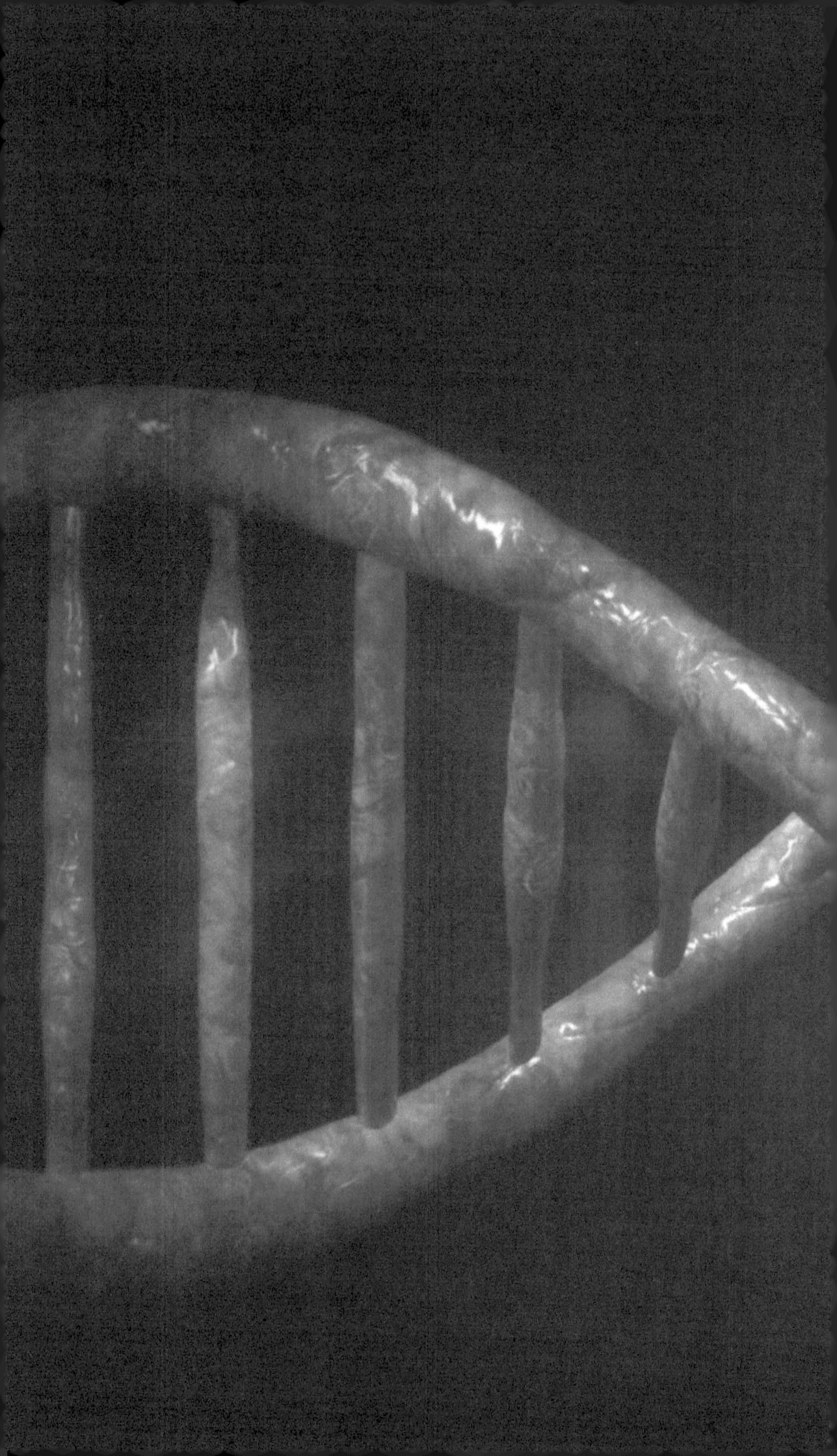

Chapter 5

Caleb

She fucking hates me. I haven't seen her since we were teenagers and I was leaving for college, but the disdain is obvious. The last time I saw her, she was a gawky teen and screaming at me about how I ruined her life.

It doesn't seem very bad. In fact, she looks like she's doing quite well for herself.

And she fills out her jeans a lot better than the last time I saw her. Her dark ponytail reaches between her shoulders and sways with each violent jerk of her hand as she stabs her finger into Levi's chest.

"Why is he here?" Her voice raises in an angry whisper. More than loud enough for me to hear every syllable.

"I told you, Sarah. He's the reason we're here." Levi's dark hair matches hers, it's just short and spiky from running his hand through it.

"That doesn't mean he has to stay with us." Her hands go on her hips, pulling in the loose fabric of her tee shirt and accentuating her waist.

I didn't know I'd enjoy the view this much.

"Sarah. He's my best friend. It's not up to you." Levi steps past her to move to the back of her Subaru. "Now, do you have shit that needs to come in?"

Sarah flashes her squinted green eyes at me before turning and following Levi.

"Good to see you too, Sarah." I try to flash her my best smile.

I might just let them figure it out. What did I do to piss her off so badly?

Another ping on my phone distracts me from the siblings quietly screaming at each other behind the hatchback.

More reports through the CDC. Violent outbursts. Random attacks. Riots in homeless camps in the heart of L.A.

The joke used to be that only Florida had these problems. Now it's nationwide.

It's spreading and who knows when it will stop. Mainstream media hasn't picked up yet that most of the occurrences are related.

Another couple of weeks, someone will put everything together. By then, it might be too late.

"Whatever." Sarah stomps past me without raising her eyes.

Levi saunters up to me with two large plastic totes stacked between his arms. "Dude. You really jacked her up." His lopsided grin reminds me of when we were kids and he had just landed a jump with his bike.

"I don't know what the hell she's so mad about. Please, enlighten me." Grabbing the top box, I follow him to the stairs.

His shoulders shake as he laughs. "Caleb, I don't even think *she* knows."

"How can someone stay cranky for ten years without a reason?" My cell vibrates in my pocket. I bet with another barrage of alerts.

A flash of his blue eyes rolling tugs my cheeks up in a grin. "You don't know her very well, do you? Sarah can hold onto something like a pit bull, good or bad."

"Levi?" Her voice rolls down the stairs as we step into the house.

"Yea?" Levi's baritone echoes in the vaulted ceiling of the large living room.

"Someone's shit is in my room!" A thump follows. Did she stomp her foot again? She almost looked cute when she did it outside.

Why would I ever think she's adorable?

"Ah, fuck." He turns to me. "Is it yours? I really hope it's yours." He drops the tote at the bottom of the banister to wipe his face.

I know which room is the guest room. It's always been the same since we were kids and came here for the summers. "No, you know I'm in the guest suite at the end of the hall."

"Goddamn it." His bronzed skin pales and he bypasses the main living area to the study door behind the stairs.

Pausing to take a deep breath, he raps lightly on the mahogany wood. "Jess, you have stuff in Sarah's room."

I wish I had popcorn. This last week I've seen her throw more temper tantrums than any toddler on television. At first it was unnerving seeing a grown woman screaming and tossing things. Now, it's becoming the daily entertainment.

"There is no walk-in closet in this hell-hole, Levi!" That shrill shriek could peel paint.

"We're in the master suite, Jess. It has tons of storage. I'm putting your things in it." He strides past me still standing with the plastic container in my hands.

Picking up the one off of the floor, he starts taking the stairs two at a time.

I don't want to miss the fireworks, so I match his pace behind him.

Light purple walls and a broad window do little to lighten the dark expression Sarah has on her face.

Clothes are everywhere. It's like a high end fashion show projectile vomited on every surface.

Sarah stands in the center near the foot of the bed with her hands on her hips. Her eyebrows lower further when she sees me step into the doorframe.

"For fuck's sake, Levi. What is this?" She waves her hand making her backpack leaning against her leg shift and fall flat onto the hardwood floor.

"It's Jessica's. I'll get it all moved. Sorry, I didn't know she did this." Levi drops his box and starts shoving dresses and shirts into a pile. "Caleb, could you—"

He's interrupted by a heavy clicking from behind us that ends with a red cheeked Jessica bursting into the room.

Those must be six inch stilettos. How does she even walk in those?

"Do *not* wrinkle those! They are dry clean *only,* Levi. There is no room in that ghastly closet. Besides, she doesn't need all of this space." Pivoting on one impossibly thin heel, she twirls her blonde hair until her long fingernail points at Sarah's chest. "You have, what, three pairs of jeans and a ratty tee shirt?" Her painted pink lips fatten into an exaggerated pout. "Oh, poor people are used to less space. You'll be fine."

Watching Sarah's neck flush and her jaw tighten, my amusement fades to anger on her behalf. "How much do you make, Jessica?" I can't help it. She needs to be taken down a notch.

"Levi is a *doctor.*" She narrows her eyes as she flashes a glare in my direction.

"I didn't ask about him. I asked about you." I'm trying very hard to keep my tone even.

Catching a glimpse of a smile on Sarah's full lips encourages me.

"Do you even have a job?" I make sure to lean against the doorframe, trapping her in the room.

Levi pauses in gathering the clothes to watch her.

"I have over three hundred thousand followers. That's worth more than money." Her honey blonde hair flips back with a practiced swat of her hand.

"Ah, I see. So, you're broke without Levi." Setting the tote near a dresser, I gather the armful of clothes from Levi.

Oops. Did I mean to drop them on the floor?

Of course I did.

"Gah! Are you going to let him treat me this way?" Her shoe makes a double tap when she stomps while gesturing wildly at Levi.

Crumpling her garments in a ball, I back into the hall so he can leave.

Jessica forces herself out and disappears in the direction of the study.

My antics win me a small smile from Sarah. Her green eyes lighten to an emerald sparkle with the reflection of the lights.

"I swear Levi, what the fuck you see in her baffles me." She picks up her bag and tosses it onto the bed. The corner of a laptop pokes out.

"I told you, her dad got me the residency through a charity event. I owed him." His voice is muffled behind the pile of frills and laces he carries down the hall to his room.

"I'd say that debt is paid, with interest!" Sarah pushes her door closed. There's still a "KEEP OUT" sign stuck to it with yellowing tape.

Levi shakes his head when he drops his armful on the big king bed. "How long do we have to stay here?"

I double the size of the pile and then sit on the edge of the mattress, leaning against the mountain of clothes.

Maybe I'll get lucky and wrinkle every damned shirt.

"With the notifications coming through, it's widespread and just catching steam. The CDC hasn't connected the dots publicly yet. I doubt they'll make an announcement until it's almost too late. They don't want to admit that a virulent form of rabies is loose. Some of the reports coming in are saying that the incubation times are getting shorter, too. That means less time to track and isolate." When I pull my phone out of my pocket, it's filled with a long scroll of alerts.

This is only going to get worse before it gets better.

"When do you think it will end?" Levi collapses into a leather bound chair and threads his fingers behind his head. He crosses his knee over the other and lets his dark hiking boot dangle. "We can't stay here forever. I have a practice to get back to."

I flash the screen at him and flip through just a section of the notifications. "We aren't anywhere close. How long can we last here if the grid fails?"

His hands fly from behind his head as he bends forward. "The what? There's no way it will get that bad, Caleb. The government will get involved before then."

I wish he wasn't so naive. "Levi, they've been involved. They seized the research right after I left." My fingers dig through my beard and scratch my cheek. The whiskers are getting longer, but I don't care.

"Aren't they doing anything?" His knee bounces as he watches me, his blue eyes dig into my skin.

"I'm sure they're gathering in the bases, calling their reserves, securing critical personnel. But, as far as stopping it? Nope, it's beyond the means of containment now. All they plan on doing is riding it out." It's what I hope to do.

"What the hell, Caleb? This really is the end?" He slumps against the chair and covers his eyes. "I should have married Penelope," he grumbles into his hand.

"I heard she married a cattle farmer in Montana after college." She's a redheaded spitfire. I tried to get a date with her back in high school after Levi dumped her, but she wouldn't talk to me. Those long pigtails were the source of many wet dreams when I was a teenager. They would have made ideal handles.

"Lucky bastard. That girl could suck start a semi truck. And skin a deer." He waves his hand towards the hall. "Jess can't even cook. I picked the wrong chick for the world to fall, man."

"Back to the grid. Is there a gen-set here? Solar?" It's easy to fall into "what if's". I wish I knew what pissed Sarah off so I could go back and change it. This isn't going to be fun to be in a battle of the sexes in the apocalypse.

"There's a generator. I'd have to see when the last fuel delivery was. I haven't been up here since I met Jess." He groans and stands up. "Let's go check the barn and sheds.

We might need to see what tools are on site and think about another supply run."

He reaches the top of the stairs ahead of me, just as Sarah steps out of her room.

She's changed into a pair of short cut off denim jeans that bring back every boy hood fantasy of daisy dukes in a rush.

I try to look away, but her cool fingers touch my arm and I freeze.

"Thank you for sticking up for me." Her big green eyes meet mine and she gives a small smile. Vanilla and cinnamon linger as she turns and bounces down the stairs in bare feet before disappearing into the kitchen.

Maybe the end of civilization won't be so bad.

Chapter 6

Jessica

This is hell. Absolutely the worst. I think my life may be over. No human should ever have to undergo this form of torture.

"What the fuck are you pouting about now?" Levi drops onto the couch next to me and pops the top on a can of beer.

Like a hillbilly.

"My post about how primitive it is here only got thirty two likes. It should be a thousand! Don't you understand how horrible this is?" Waving my hand in front of my eyes might help to dry the welling tears before they smear my mascara.

"You're joking, right?" He scrolls through his phone, ignorant of the trauma I am experiencing. "A third hospital has shut down in L.A.. The mayor said they are instilling martial law. I hear the president is even talking about implementing it."

"I don't care what the president is doing unless he's liking my posts." Maybe I should take a picture of how much it is ruining me that no one is commenting. That should get me some sympathy reactions.

"Jess, do you have any idea how shallow you are? People are dying." He turns his screen to show me some ghastly video of two people eating someone in a street.

"Ew, Levi. Keep your creepy horror movie garbage to yourself. I am doing important work!" A whirring sound from the kitchen catches my ear.

Perfect.

My skirt is tight, so I take small, rapid steps from the living room to catch Sarah working the espresso machine.

"Make me one, too." It's exhausting walking in these heels. Sliding into one of the barstools, I let out an extra long sigh. She needs to know how tired I am.

"I'm not your personal assistant." She wipes the nozzle down and pours some milk from a can into it.

It's a true struggle to not wrinkle my nose.

"You're so much better at it than I am." I'm glad my mascara didn't run. It wouldn't look as genuine batting my lashes at her.

"That shit doesn't work on me. Make your own. And do the dishes for fuck's sake. Everyone else pitches in." She brushes past me and pulls the screen door open to the porch.

"I just did my nails! Do you have any idea how long it took to do that? I can't get them wet." Everyone is against me.

She has the audacity to scoff at me before letting the door slam shut behind her.

Bitch.

Screw the coffee.

"Levi! I want to go home!" I find him back on the couch and push myself between his knees. "Please?" How far can I stick out my lower lip?

"Jess. It isn't safe. That wasn't a movie I was showing you." He's slouched against the cushions and not even looking at me.

"Levi, poor people have been shitting in the streets forever. They'll do anything to get on television. I want to go home." Poking out my chest, I let one of my long nails trace down his leg. "Come on, baby. I'll make it worth your while."

His blue eyes fix on me and he raises one eyebrow. "You're really willing to whore yourself out to go back? The last time you let me touch you was when you wanted that beamer." His jaw clenches and his lips thin. "Don't fuck with me, or I'll bend you over, have my way, then lock you in the basement until I'm bored with you."

"You're such an asshole." My makeup crinkles in the corners of my eyes at the disgusting thought of the dank storage downstairs. "I miss my friends. I want a soy chai latte from Cafe Solie. The canned milk freaks me out, Levi. This place is not for me, I'm going."

"I pulled the spark plugs in all the cars, Jess. You're not leaving until I know it's safe." He crosses his ankle over his knee, effectively barring me from his groin.

"I hate you! Fix it and let me go!" My shoe makes a double tap when I stomp my foot. I wish I could slap him.

"How about you earn it? Help out here for a week and I'll take you to town. We could use some more supplies anyways." His lips fall into a lopsided grin, framed by a week's worth of dark beard.

He's almost cute when he's being a dick. "How am I supposed to do that?" Please let it be just pushing my tits up. "I help best by staying out of the way."

"That would be almost better than what you do now. Go change into real clothes and not your busy body shit. Ditch the heels. Do the dishes like Sarah asked. Maybe your own laundry? We aren't your personal wait staff." His smile disappears into a look of cold indifference. "I'm just asking you to pull your weight."

Does he really care that little for me? He wants me to do menial work? "You're a horrible husband for not taking care of me!"

"Jesus, fuck. I'm saving your ungrateful life. Things are worse than Caleb predicted, but we're safe here. Would you rather be home and dead? Or worse? Look at what the infected do!" He flashes his phone at me showing a shaky video of some half dressed woman with blood running down her shirt.

My god, she's chewing on her own arm.

"That isn't real, Levi!" It can't be. Even if it is, she must be high on some cheap street drug.

"Fine. Call your friends. Get them each on the phone and I'd bet there's some you can't reach. They're already estimating that by the end of the week nearly ten percent of the population will have it." Sliding his cell into his shirt pocket, he leans forward and grabs my upper arms roughly. "Phil, Steve and their wives all got it. They're dead, Jessica."

"Your partners? How? They're plastic surgeons! We're in the one percent, Levi. That's a long way from the bottom ten." I can't imagine Phil with his perfect smile and his Lamborghini chewing on his own arm.

"One percent in income does not mean we're automatically immune." His fingers dig into me as he pushes me to the side. "I need another beer. Earn your trip or not. I don't care."

The screen door pops at the same time as Levi brushes past me to the kitchen. Caleb pushes in with a grocery bag full of something that looks wet.

"Levi! I caught a bunch of trout down at the lake." He pulls a slimy fish out of the sack and the smell wafts over me making my stomach turn.

"Ew. I am *not* eating that." I think I'm going to be sick.

Caleb glances at me and his dark eyes narrow. "I wasn't offering. You're welcome to clean one if you get hungry."

Ugh, everyone here is horrible to me.

"I can help." Sarah pushes through the screen door and follows him around the counter. "I've been working on getting some plants started for a garden. The fish guts will make good fertilizer."

Caleb smiles at her and I want to vomit.

Dirt. Guts. Canned milk.

I'm in some sort of backwoods nightmare.

Absolutely primitive.

"Sarah, do you know if Mom's cornbread recipe is floating around? That would taste amazing with some pan-fried filets." Levi reaches into one of the cupboards and pulls out a red and white checkered book with a big pot on the cover.

He looks up, his blue eyes fixing on me. "Jessica, why don't you be a good girl and go fetch some of the corn meal from the basement." His gaze is unwavering.

Shit. He's serious.

"Fine. I'll be your little bitch." If he wants me to be a servant, I might even put on some sneakers.

The book slaps against the counter as his body tenses over it. "With that attitude, you're going to get it doggie style." His lips twist into a sarcastic smirk.

Sarah snorts and her face turns red.

Caleb lets out a deep laugh that carries through the house.I can still hear him as I hurry down the hall to the study that I've claimed as my retreat.

I hate them all.

My adorable penny loafers are the only highlight of this miserable day. I bought them at a chic couture shop just off of Hollywood Boulevard and I haven't worn them since.

Look at me, I'm being sensible. I bet they would pair well with a plaid skirt and white blouse. Maybe Levi would take me seriously then. Or, at least be swayed more easily.

I'll be the naughty schoolgirl if it gets me out of this hovel. He wants me to go into the disgusting basement, fine. The stairs creak and the musty smell works its way up my body with every degree that drops as I step lower beneath the house. It's cold enough to make goosebumps erupt on my arms.

Fuck, I hope I don't stink like mothballs.

There are buckets marked with flour, oats, sugar and more. I swear there's enough here to feed us for months.

Oh no.

I can't do this for another day, much less half a year or more. Literally worse than death.

But, if there wasn't so much food, we'd have to leave sooner.

The lid on the closest bucket is stuck on so tightly, I can't pry it up. So is the next. A funny 'T' shaped tool hangs from the wall on a gray nail. It seems like it would work to open one, but I am not dressed to get dirty.

A small plastic container labeled "corn meal" is sitting on a shelf.

I think I can do what Levi asked. I'll earn my keep. And, I'll have him teach me how to open these buckets.

We get hungry enough, we'll have to go back to town.

Chapter 7

Sarah

I can't help it, he's growing on me.

When he stood up to Jessica for me, it's like a little bubble popped inside my chest. Maybe he isn't so bad.

We've all fallen into a routine. Breakfast is usually a bit of fend for ourselves since we all seem to survive on only coffee.

Lunch and dinner have become group activities. Well, for three out of four of us.

It really is better when Jessica stays the fuck out of the way. I hate this new kick she's on where she's trying to learn, but she's so damned stupid she ruins the food more often than not.

"I swear, she couldn't do worse if she was actually trying to screw up." Seriously. I'm on my hands and knees cleaning up the gallon jug of maple syrup she "accidently" pushed off of the counter and walked away from.

Over an hour went by before Caleb discovered it. At least he's helping me wipe it up.

"It'd be nice if she were to try harder and just pitch it straight into the garbage instead of this crap." His grumble turns into a growl of frustration as he lowers his shoulders to pull syrup from under the fridge.

His ass is sticking up right in front of me and I can see the bulge in his bright red shorts hanging between his lean thighs.

Shit, I have to stop staring at him.

What started as abject hatred has tempered to a mild irritation.

I think we've bonded over our mutual hatred and disgust of Jessica.

"Why isn't she here cleaning this up? She could at least help, even if it wasn't on purpose." My rag is so saturated with the sticky goo I can't peel it out of my hand.

"I'm good with her not being here." Caleb's voice is low, probably so Levi or Jess won't hear him.

I don't care if they hear me. It's my house too.

"It's kinda bullshit, Caleb. We aren't her personal wait staff. But, I do agree with her on one thing, how much longer do we have to stay here?" The pan I've been ladling syrup into is full. When I stand up, he's still hunched on his knees with one arm pulling the tarry liquid from under the cupboard.

Why do I have the ridiculous idea to swat his ass?

Damned intrusive thoughts.

Hot water still takes a long time to flush the cake pan clean and my eyes wander out the big window above the sink.

I can just see the tips of my vegetables growing in the garden. By next month it will be a wall of green.

Another four weeks with Jessica, she'll be buried out there next to the cucumbers. She's driving me crazy.

"I've heard blood meal makes the best fertilizer for tomatoes." Caleb pushes into the sink next to me, his large hands covered with a maple glaze. He gestures with his forehead as he robs the spigot from me.

Flashing a white smile just inches from me, he leans over and puts his lips almost against my ear.

A flurry of electricity runs up my spine as I feel his whiskers tickle against my cheek. "How big would the hole need to be to fit her in it?" With a soft chuckle, he turns away and flicks his wet fingers into the sink.

My jaw drops in feigned horror in a pathetic attempt to cover up what I'm really thinking.

What was that? I shouldn't *like* it when he got so close.

"I'd have world class tomatoes with all of the bullshit she's full of." Chewing on my bottom lip manages to hold back the laugh that's dying to escape.

He leans his back against the counter, the small hand towel knotting around his fingers as his dark eyes fix on my mouth. They crinkle as a hint of a smile flickers through his beard and he leans towards me again.

In my space.

"You know—" His voice drops to a low whisper and another warm shiver runs through me. "—that would make us conspirators. Can you keep a secret that big?" His hot breath caresses my shoulder and winds around my neck.

Heat rushes to my cheeks as I silently will my heart not to race so fast.

I don't back away, but turn to face him. I can see my reflection in the bottomless chestnut colored pits of his eyes. "I can keep a secret. Can you?"

Why does it feel like I'm not talking about murder anymore, but something even more nefarious?

The heat of his chest radiates into mine. My damned nipples rise to attention and I very much wish I had put on a bra under this tank top to help hide them.

"I have top clearance. You don't get that if you like to talk." His gaze drops between us before he looks back up, raising one brow into an arch.

It's a surprise when his hand closes over my shoulder, searing into my bare skin. The rough terry cloth towel drags across my collarbone and I feel the sticky pull as he wipes a drop of syrup off of me.

My lungs spasm a small gasp. "But," I splutter. "You talked to Levi." I can't breathe. I'm paralyzed by his scorching touch.

"Sarah." His nostrils flare as he drops his hand.

I feel cold without it.

"I'll break every rule to make sure the people I care about are safe." With a gentle toss, he flips the towel across the edge of the sink and steps around the counter to disappear through the screen door.

The hollow echo of the thin wood slapping against the frame knocks me from whatever spell he put me under.

Whoa. We must have been trapped together too long. It takes forever for my heart to stop racing and my body to return to a normal temperature.

***

My head is in the clouds all afternoon. Every time I hear his voice it makes my breath hitch and a weird feeling flit through my stomach.

Some time before dinner he pulled Levi off to the barn.

I keep trying to come up with excuses to go out there and see what's going on, but everything I can think of sounds corny.

So, I end up in the garden. There's some leaf lettuce, baby carrots and some beets that are big enough to thin and use for a salad. It will be nice to have something fresh. The produce ran out a couple of weeks ago. Canned and frozen just aren't the same.

When Jessica's petulant screech punctures the silence, it takes everything in me to not start digging that hole that Caleb was joking about.

Just the thought of him runs a tremble through me.

I need to stop with this craziness. Tonight I'll vent some of this frustration. That should help.

Since I didn't have a lot of help for dinner, I went for a basic baked chicken shredded over the salad.

"Finally, someone made some real food." Jessica sits with a heavy sigh. She almost snuck in without the warning clicks of her high heels preceding her. "I would kill for a balsamic vinaigrette. What is this? Ranch?" She picks up the bottle with the tips of two fingers and her eyes roll until all I see is the whites.

Like she's begging to have me run my fork into one.

"It's all we have." Taking the first mouthful, a sense of satisfaction fills me. I grew this. It's better than buying stuff at the store. Tastes better, too.

"We're living like animals." Her extended lashes flutter as she pouts when Levi walks in. "Honey, when are we going for supplies?"

Wow, she even moves the phone away from the front of her face long enough to give him a fake smile. She must really be serious.

"We were just talking about that." Caleb follows my brother into the kitchen, his deep voice rekindling an ache that's been in my belly all day.

He lets his fingers brush my back as he leans on my chair to take his own seat next to me.

Is he messing with me? Did I never notice that before, how comfortable we're getting around each other?

"Oh!" Jessica's squeal could strip paint.

"Yea, it might be worth a trip to restock before everything really takes a shit. Our stuff is going faster than I thought it would." Levi has bags under his eyes. Life with his wife twenty four hours a day looks like it's killing him.

"There's something else." Caleb glances at me as he scoops greens onto his plate. "Some preliminary research is showing that people who have received the rabies vaccine seem to not develop extreme symptoms. I found a veterinary clinic nearby that still has a few doses left. It took some convincing, but I want to make sure you all get some."

"If I get one of your shots, does that mean we can go home?" Jessica pushes her bare salad around on her plate before aiming her cell at it to take a picture. "I'll volunteer."

I didn't expect that.

"Yes, fine. I'll make arrangements." Levi looks defeated. I bet he's regretting his life choices right about now.

I tried to tell him. It doesn't matter now though.

"If everyone is in agreement, we have some coordinating to do. The vet wants supplies in exchange." Caleb nods to Levi before continuing. "So we need to get some more for him. If we give him what's here, we'll run out too quickly. It would go fastest with all four of us working together." He lifts his glass of water and his Adam's apple bobs with every swallow.

Why am I just now noticing the veins in his arms and the way the muscles flex beneath his skin?

Because I wasn't this horny before.

Maybe a change of scenery would be good.

"I'm game. We'll need supplies anyways. As crappy as things are getting according to the news, we're gonna need to be in for the long haul." I start making a mental list of everything I'd like to bring back.

Why are condoms the first thing I think of? I need a vibrator.

Squeezing my legs together to try and calm the twitching going on between them, I lose focus when Jessica starts talking about all of the stores she wants to go to.

Her incessant noise is still going on as Caleb leans back and stretches his legs out beneath the table. His foot lands on mine and he tosses me a small 'o' face of surprise before moving it.

It doesn't stop the jolt that sizzles through me.

"So, Sarah." He weaves his fingers behind his head, framing his face with his biceps. "How are those tomatoes coming along?"

Shit, I snort and water shoots from my nose. I did *not* expect that.

"We'll have grand champions in no time." I can't hide my grin as I wipe my face.

Levi stands up, interrupting Jessica. "We aren't going to any of them. So just shut the fuck up." He grabs his plate and stomps to the sink, tossing it in with a clatter before storming outside.

"What is wrong with him?" She bats her blue eyes that are open impossibly wide.

"You." The tingle in my belly shifts to nausea at how miserable she makes my brother. If I had known it was going to be this bad for him, I would have thrown a bigger fit at his wedding.

Her eyes narrow as she throws her fork down. "Well, your salad is gross." She grabs her phone and shoves her chair away from the table before disappearing down the hall.

The study door slams, rattling the house.

"She makes gnawing my own arm off sound like an option." Caleb reaches across the table and gathers Jessica's abandoned plate then places it on his own.

He smells faintly like old leather as he stands, holding his palm out.

"Oh, thank you." Our fingers brush as I hand him my dishes.

There's that quiver again. His narrow waist is at eye level and his bright red shorts make it hard not to look at them.

His chest rumbles a sound of approval before he steps past me to turn on the faucet. "Thanks for making dinner, it was good. The salad was a wonderful change."

I catch his profile as he looks out the window. There's a soft curl to his hair that's just touching his ears. His strong jaw is almost hidden beneath his dark beard. The way his shirt hangs, I can just make out the definition in his chest. And those shorts hug over that ass like he could drive a nail with those cheeks.

Eyes back on the table, Sarah. You are *not* hot for Caleb.

Remember what he did to you?

Barely. Was it really that bad? Or am I just holding a grudge unnecessarily because I had my feelings hurt as a teenager.

Probably.

"Thank you for doing the dishes." The last of the condiments go back to the fridge and I busy myself with wiping the table down once it's empty.

It's like I don't want to leave.

No. Not going to happen.

"Any time. You're a good cook, I'd be happy to clean up after any meal you make." He flashes me a broad smile.

Dang, he is pretty cute.

Fuck. Okay, he's gorgeous.

Ugh, I need to get out of here. "You're sweet. Have a good night, Caleb."

"G'night." He turns and glances at me before looking back to his hands in the frothy water.

Did he just wink at me?

I must have imagined it.

My feet are heavy as I head upstairs to my room. Maybe I'll check my emails, I haven't done that for a few days.

Wow. There's a ton of old ones, but not many new ones. Most are from the school. First addresses the growing number of absences. Then there are some about the teacher shortages. The last few are about district closures.

They shut them down? How did I miss that on the notifications on my phone?

It looks like I don't have to worry about going back to work any time soon. There's no end date.

When is this going to end? Will everyone eventually get it? Is it safe to leave?

Every day is more questions and less answers.

Like, why am I holding out when I know I could enjoy myself with Caleb? I've known him forever and he's proven himself a good guy here. What is stopping me besides my own stubborn pride?

Oh yea, me.

I'm done with the laptop. I can't handle any more doom and gloom tonight.

The hall is empty when I sneak out to use the bathroom.

After my nightly routine is complete, I slide between my cool sheets and stare at the moonlight on my wall. The posters from when I was younger cast eerie shadows that make my mind wander.

Before I can stop myself, I think about Caleb's hand gripping my shoulder and how close his lips were to mine.

What would he taste like? I'm dying to see what's hidden beneath his shirt. To touch him, trace my hands down his chest.

Mine mimic my thoughts, trailing down my breasts with a light tickle until I push my fingers beneath the hem of my panties.

I'm soaked with the image of him holding me, caressing me. I can almost feel the weight of his body over mine, the brush of his beard against my neck.

God, he'd growl in my ear as he pushed into me.

My finger finds my clit and I furiously stroke myself, hoping it will magically turn into him plunging into me, filling me, screaming my name.

His leaves my lips as I moan into the crook of my elbow, a shuddering release rippling through my belly.

Heat spreads through my limbs and I melt into my pillow.

Maybe that's all I needed to get him out of my head.

Chapter 8

Peter

I don't even bother hiding anymore. The cops have disappeared. I haven't seen a patrol car in weeks.

No one is cleaning up the dead bodies. Except the infected. They're having their feasts on every corner, in every alley.

We've all become immune to the screams.

When I went back to my old apartment, all of my shit was gone.

Big surprise.

The old bitch that runs the place wasn't home, so I let myself in and took what I needed. I knew she had a gun somewhere, it didn't take long to find it. And more cash than I thought she deserved.

Not like it does any good anymore. Most of the grocery stores are running empty. The trucks aren't coming into the city. I heard something about drivers getting ripped from their cabs and eaten on the curb while the food in the back was devoured at the same time.

Surf and turf, L.A. style.

The weird part is, I've been bit twice more since the hospital, but I haven't turned into one of those mindless mouths running around the streets.

I have zero clue why. The wounds heal within a day, too.

It's almost like magic. I cut my palm open once, to test it. By the time I grabbed a rag to wipe the blood away, the slice was already pulling itself together without a scar.

I'm fucking bullet-proof.

I bet being shot would still hurt a fuck-ton. But if it doesn't kill me, I bet I'd survive.

The noises in the streets are getting a little tiresome, though. I think today I'll take a jaunt north into some of the suburbs to see if I can find a nicer place to crash for a while.

I've never felt more free. It took me a few weeks of hiding before I even showed my face. Usually the police don't like escapees running around.

Looks bad for them.

Last night was the first one I really felt like I wasn't going to get caught. I finally got to vent some of this pressure that has been building inside of me.

I don't know how that petite blonde ended up alone on a street full of monsters, dodging the grasping hands that tried to pull her into the shadows.

She's lucky I rescued her. I can't imagine if she had been caught by one of them. Her screams would have been much louder than the fearful mewling she made when I held her down.

If only she wasn't a whore. Her innocence was gone.

But, damn it felt good to sink my cock in a cunt versus my own fist. Used is better than none.

She squeezed me so tight as I choked her. I'll remember how her hips bucked against me and her brown eyes bulged. That moment when the blood vessels break and the whites are flooded with red makes me hard just thinking about it.

She died better. Barely a noise at all.

I didn't need a condom. Not when the disposal units are prowling the streets in search of food. They almost turned on me as I drug her limp body into the sidewalk. But, when they saw what I offered, they had her torn apart in moments.

Well, there is a stain. I did see a kid licking it this morning. It was a rare sight, like a robin on a winter morning. Children have been scarce lately. That one must be wily to avoid being eaten.

Gotta be tough nowadays and I feel invincible. The sun is bright and warm on my shoulders, I got laid last night, and I can't be injured.

The world is mine.

Brazenly carrying a pistol across my chest and a shotgun nestled in the crook of my elbow, I dare anyone to try and fuck with me.

Sporadic gunshots echo around me. Distance is hard to judge as the sounds ricochet through the brick walls of the buildings.

Someone is fighting back. There might be a few who survive.

The manicured lawns fade into unkempt tangles of weeds and garbage. Ah, the gives-zero-shits community marker.

A flash of something white hints through the waving brush.

What the hell? It looks like a white beach ball that is moving.

Chewing. The crunches grow louder as I get closer.

"Well, aren't you the fattest fuck I've ever seen." I bet she's seven hundred pounds, wheezing on all fours.

She bends over the ripped entrails of what looks like a labrador and shoves it into her mouth, her rippling rolls quivering with each bite.

Weeping sores dot her back and dimpled ass cheeks as the smell of damp rot hits me. Every time she moves, her fat folds glisten with an off white sickly sweet grainy fluid. It's like fetid ricotta that oozes between each crease.

She pays me no mind as I sink my fingers between the undulating hills of her side. Her ribs have long hidden under the gelatinous tissue.

It's soft, moist, like her body is covered in whorish cunts begging to be ripped open. She smells like some of those prostitutes that wandered under the overpasses.

I tried to do my part. No one cared when they went missing. At least they knew how to get me off after the lure of a baggie was dangled from my fingers. The ones with no teeth were my favorites. When I'd run the screwdriver through their temples as they sucked me off, it made their jaw clamp so fucking tight they almost would gum my cock off.

A delicious shiver runs up my spine.

I can't help myself. Unzipping my pants, I rub the tip of my hardening cock against the crusty fluid and rock against her as she sloppily shoves a bulbous piece of organ into her mouth.

"You're such a nasty dog. You've got enough in reserves to live for months." I wonder what she would look like skinnier. Standing over her back with my dick in my hand, my bowie knife reflects the glint of the gorgeous day until I bury it between the edge of her chest and the extra flesh that covers it.

A crimson river erupts as I drag it down, fileting her form from the thick yellow layer of clinging flab.

Rolling my tongue against the roof of my mouth, I loose a piercing whistle. "Just gonna call some of your friends, Lassie."

She gives a shrill moan, but stuffs another handful into her drooling round maw.

A matching slice on the other side leaves her with two pillows of skin and pus-like fat spilling away from her like quivering wings.

Shuffling feet announce two newcomers. Both women and barely clothed, their gaunt and sunken eyes first latch on me before the hunger awakens as they see the massive meal in front of them.

God, three at once. My nuts start to twitch as my strokes on my cock get faster.

Their fingers tear into the open sides of the bleeding mass. When the older one falls to her knees to bury her face in the puddle of blood, the short tattered dress flies up to reveal her torn panties.

And, her bare pussy.

My day just got better.

With her slurping and sucking on the congealing tissue beneath her, I slip my raging cock into her dry cunt.

I pull out just enough to let a long string of saliva land on my hard shaft before plunging back in.

She doesn't even react until I grab a fistful of her hair and jerk her head up. Dropping her shoulders just drives me deeper as her mouth gapes to pull more of the fatty meat in.

"That's it, eat, baby." Knotting my fingers into her tangled braid, I force her nose and mouth into the fetid mess of chunky tissue.

Her arms jerk as she struggles to breath, but her movements are sporadic, uncoordinated.

There it is. That moment when her body seizes as it suffocates, clamping down on my cock. My nuts spasm and I lose myself, spurting hot ribbons as the tremors of her walls lessen.

When I unthread my fingers and unsheath myself, her hips sink as her chest slides into the red gore of fatty still tearing away at the hip muscle of the dog.

I'm just tucking my softening cock into my pants when the bowels on my cum bucket loosen. Brown and white fluids mix into a putrid mess with the yellow and crimson tide on the sidewalk.

I made a fucking rainbow. Just needs maybe a bit of blue.

That might work. Sitting outside of the garage door are a couple of jugs of motor oil. Not exactly blue, but would add a few more iridescent colors.

The bottles are blue. When they melt, it will add to the palette.

Heavy globs of the thick sludge pours over the back of the two consuming bitches that are still more focused on stuffing their faces than anything I'm doing.

I'll even throw on some sticks and paper. Look at that, I'm tidying up the yard.

The flames start slow, neither one paying any attention to the fact that I'm coaxing a campfire on their asses.

When the exposed fat catches, it wicks into the cardboard and paper.

Now I have a nice little blaze.

Possibilities start spinning through my head. No one gives a shit now. I'm here, in the open, on the street of a residential neighborhood.

I can do anything I want. I can be king.

They eat until their skin is too charred for their arms to move. Only then do they start making a low keening sound as the sizzle of cooking meat fills the afternoon air.

Smells good. I'm kinda craving steak and marshmallows now.

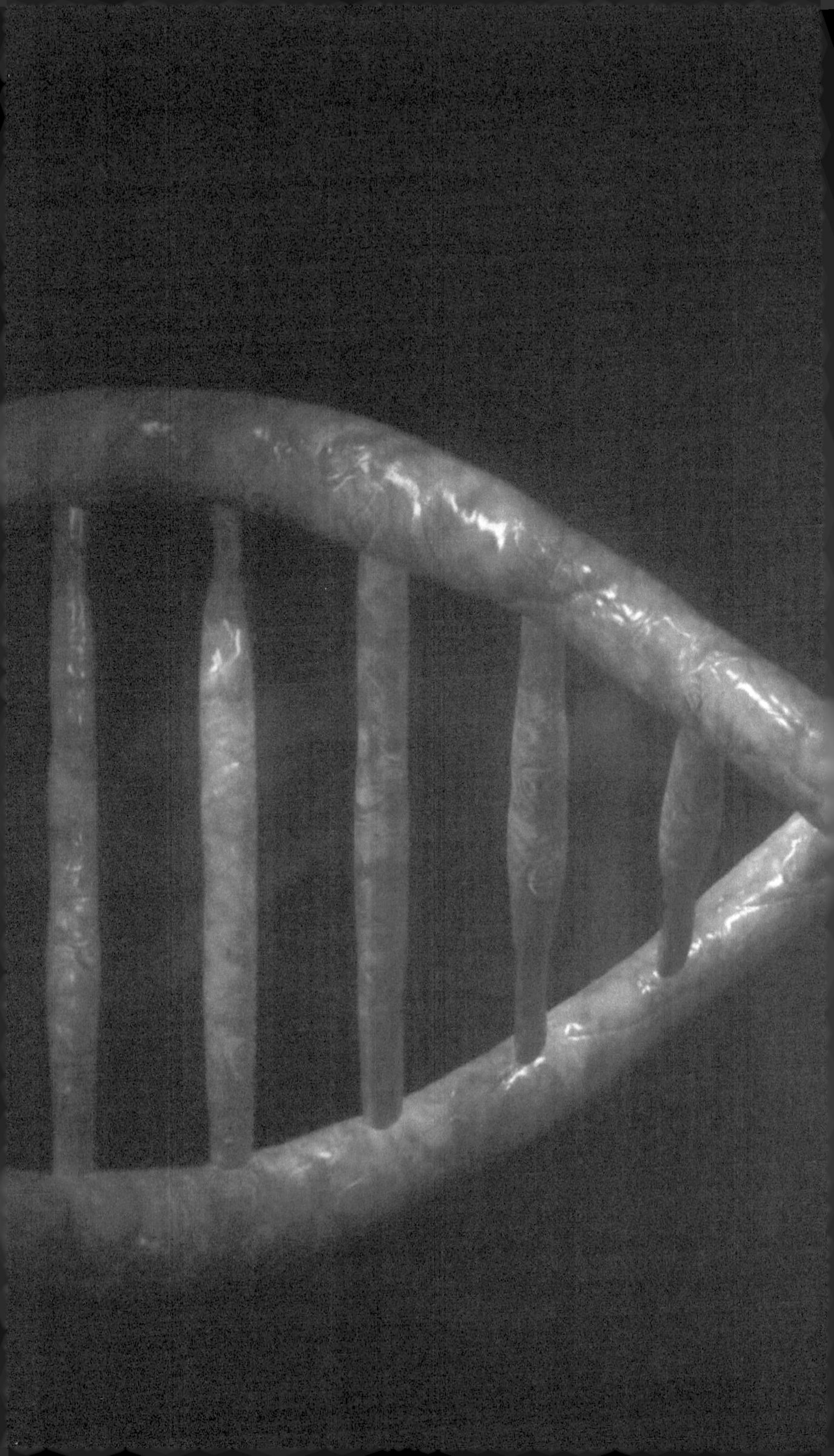

Chapter 9
Caleb

Hearing her soft moans through the wall followed by my name with her breathy cries had me fisting myself until I came all over my sheets.

Like a damned teenager.

I almost busted in her door. I'm sure that would be a great impression. It's taken me weeks to get her to not glower at me most of the time. Slowly winning her over has been my personal goal.

After all, we may need to repopulate the earth soon.

Won't happen by fucking my own hand.

The thought of her belly round with my baby makes my cock hard as granite with my fingers still covered in my own sticky fluids.

There's no way I can sleep. I'd have to get off a dozen times in the hope that those sounds fade from my memory long enough to pass out.

We're safe here in the woods. Far from the threats of the cities, it'd be easy to build a life to ride out the virus. If we could get to town and restock with the intention of being out here years instead of months, all we'd have to do is live and fuck until there's a sea of kids.

My teeth sink into my arm as I try to swallow down a groan.

Our children. It could happen.

I just need to get my cock in her and show her how good it can be.

***

She has to be wearing that on purpose to torture me. Her soft teal tank top makes her eyes almost glow in the morning light pouring through the bay windows.

But, I don't care about her eyes. It's the low cut that flirts with the edge of her bra that holds my attention. Her cleavage is calling for me to bury my nose and taste what she's covering.

Those shorts don't help. Cut off denim that cups her ass every time she crosses the room to the coffee maker.

Knowing it was my name on her lips is making this difficult to carry on a shallow, light hearted conversation about what she wants to do in the garden today.

I can't tell her what I'd rather be doing.

"Does that sound good?" Her full cup is nestled between her palms as she pulls one knee to her chest, perching her bare foot on the edge of her wooden chair.

Those green eyes fix on me over the rim as she takes a slow sip.

"Um, sure." I have no idea what she just asked me. The memory of her moan is on repeat. "Can you detail out what you wanted?"

My own drink is gone. I don't know if I can stand and make it past the counter without her seeing my dick bulging in my shorts.

Jeans would have been a better choice.

She drops her leg and leans her elbows on the table, squeezing her glorious orbs between her arms as a smile teases over her lips. "Well—" She rolls her bottom lip between her teeth. "—there's some wood in the barn I'd like to turn into planters so I can put some plastic over them and extend the growing season. I think we're going to be here longer than we thought." Her mouth lowers into a pout as she looks down at her cup.

Her fingers dance over the rim of her mug in a light circle.

What would they feel like if they were circling the head of my aching dick?

She's killing me.

My palm finds my stiff crotch to try to force my length into my waistband. Using the table as a shield from her view, I'm almost tempted to stroke myself.

At this rate, I'll have to sneak away to the bathroom before much longer.

"Levi! Make me a coffee!" Jessica's shrill voice shatters the tranquil peace.

Well, that'll kill a hard-on.

"Yea, I'll be happy to help. Good excuse to get out of the house." I flash her a pained grin. My jaw clenches until Jessica quiets.

Levi has bags under his eyes and his cheeks look hollow as he steps through the opening from the living room to the kitchen. "I swear to fuck I'm going to kill her one of these days."

Sarah meets my glance with a suspiciously mischievous looking wink.

Jesus. Just when I was starting to go soft, blood surges back between my legs.

I've got a secret she can keep. Thrust deep inside of her.

Levi's woes are a good reminder of how relationships can go. My last girlfriend left me for her coworker. I'm pretty sure it's because he had a yacht.

Stupid me, I was saving up for her dream wedding.

"Everything all right there, buddy?" A little readjustment and I risk standing up to refill my cup.

"When we go back to town, I'm leaving her at the house. I don't give a shit anymore." His voice is hoarse. "I'm so sick of her constantly bitching." His hands splay on the counter and his head hangs below his shoulders. "She did it before, but we were both so busy I didn't care. I left a good piece of ass back at the office to try and do the right thing by bringing her here. Look where that got me."

"Levi, you should have just split with her if you weren't happy. Better than cheating on her, even if she is cunt." Sarah stands and slips on her flip flops.

I love her filthy mouth. She's gotten more comfortable around me the last few weeks, and her dirty mind has really shone.

And to think I always saw her as the prim and quiet one. There's a fire in her I want to engulf myself in.

"Think she'll be safer at the house, or maybe her folk's place?" As much as I dislike Jessica, I want to give her a fighting chance. Having her gone would help make things much more relaxed here.

"I don't give a fuck. I'll drop her wherever she wants me to drop her, and then she's on her own. I'm done trying." He jerks the cupboard door hard enough for it to bounce on its hinges.

"Good thing that vet said he'd meet with us in two days." Opening the fridge out of habit, it closes on its own. There's no more milk. The canned stuff ran out a while back, and the dried box got wet somehow and soured.

How hard is it to have a cow? Or a goat? We might need to start thinking long term.

I've read that goats used to be a good milk replacer for babies. If I get Sarah pregnant...

Dammit, I need to jack off before I explode.

"I wish you luck. I'm just glad she'll be gone." Sarah pulls the screen door open that leads to the porch and pauses. Her chin turns and those green eyes catch mine. "Caleb? Still want to help?"

Who am I to say no to that?

"Gladly." Levi is miserable to be around. I'd rather pursue more worthwhile company.

And it's wearing cut off shorts.

Her shoes smack against the soles of her feet in rhythm with every sway of her hips. The tease of the gap between her top and her shorts makes my fingers tingle wanting to touch her.

I don't know how much longer I can hold off. Tucking myself back into my waistband means I might not inadvertently poke her.

Or scare her. It's not like I'm a small man.

My fingers run through my hair. The world is going to shit and all I can think about is getting laid.

There's worse things.

The heat of the morning sun fades as we step into the dim door of the barn. Light filters through dusty windows, enough to be able to see easily.

"So, how much longer do you think the plastic will help to extend the growing season?" I need to distract myself. Moving boxes off of the pile of lumber keeps me occupied.

"I'm hoping for at least another two months. It should be enough for some fall crops of beans, beets, and other stuff that should last. Having Jess out of here would probably save us a ton. She seems to break or drop something almost daily." Her lips thin as she takes one of the totes from me. "Do you think she's doing it on purpose?"

"I have no doubt. She wants out of here. Your brother has the patience of a saint." I honestly feel bad for him. He doesn't even seem to like her, why would he marry her? They obviously have nothing in common.

Well, money.

"He only thought with his pocket. Look what money bought him. A fucking nightmare." She laughs a light and airy giggle that tingles its way to my nuts.

"There's better things than riches." My fingers brush hers as I hand off a milk crate full of dusty cables. A pang of longing arcs from the contact.

"That's true." Her shirt lifts as she pushes the box onto a high shelf. "Seeing my kids learning something new and getting it. There's this beautiful moment when the light-bulb goes off and they're overwhelmed with the purest joy." Sarah purses her lips and looks toward the light spilling through the doorway. "It's really one of the best things."

"So—" I'm not sure if I should ask this, if it will be pushing too far. "—have you ever thought of having any of your own?"

Please say yes.

"Of course! I love them." A deep velvety red flush works up her neck to color her cheeks. "But, I haven't really met the right guy." The last word chokes out like it was lodged in her throat. "I mean, nowadays it's hard enough to get by. I can't imagine trying to do that with children." Her hand waves through the dusty air. "And, now with everything going on..." She trails off, shaking her head.

"What would the 'right guy' be like?" My hands sweat, but I've opened this Pandora's box, might as well follow through. "Would it be someone who helps you?" A flimsy suitcase is one of the last things on the pile that I hand to her. "Maybe, someone who works with you to clean up messes?" I hope she can see where I'm going with this.

Her teeth turn her lower lip between them as she takes the piece of luggage. "Um. That's a good start."

She isn't running away or yelling at me.

That has to be a good sign.

"Someone who stands up for you?" I know Jessica isn't much of an enemy. That was the moment when I saw something change in Sarah's eyes though.

Her nostrils flare and her eyes darken as her brows furrow. She turns away to pace across the dirty floor. "You mean, a guy who asked me for a pen to get another girl's number?"

My stomach knots. I just got sucker punched.

That's why she was mad.

"Sarah, I was nineteen. You were fourteen. Plus, you were Levi's little sister." Crap.

Her green eyes shimmer as they narrow and her hands go to her hips. "I'm still his sister. And that was his girlfriend."

I hold up my palms. "Technically, *ex*-girlfriend. They were already split. I was young and dumb." The fact that I knew she put out was a lure that was hard to avoid.

Wait. This isn't adding up.

"Why did it make you angry enough to hold a grudge against me for so long?" I drop my hands and walk slowly closer.

It's an act of nature to resist kissing her full lips as she clenches her jaw. A rainbow of emotion flickers across her features until her gaze drops and she focuses on my feet.

Please don't be my crotch. My cock is throbbing to break free.

The subtle hint of vanilla wafts over me as I move within arm's reach.

She shrugs her bare shoulders and tucks a lock of dark hair behind her ear. "I guess I had a stupid crush on you."

There it is. The truth.

Regret leaves a sour taste. If I had known what was right in front of me, I would have never squandered those years chasing the wrong women.

I'd have waited for her.

"How we feel is never wrong." It's quite a thing, standing in an old barn, wedged between racks and old vehicles, and finding out someone has been in love with me for years.

There's no other explanation for her carrying her pain and anger for so long. Surely there was someone else to put a gap in her feelings? She's never talked about it. But, she knows about my failed attempt. Levi was quite thorough in ribbing me about it over several dinners.

His words were that I was "lucky" it fell apart.

I didn't think that, until now.

"Yea, well, it hurt to be rejected. Okay, I know, you didn't do that. It was more like I wasn't even considered."

Her arms wrap around her slim waist and her gaze flicks everywhere around me.

My fingers dig into the coarse hairs on my chin. I want to touch her, to comfort her.

"Did I mention the young and dumb part? I didn't know, Sarah. I can promise, things would have been very different if I had." We'd already have children running around.

God damn it. Stop with that. She's not ready. She barely likes me, but I'm making progress.

Her palm rubs away the tears gathering in the wells of her eyes. "How?" The green is tinged with red from the friction of her hands.

And the pain she's been suffering because of me for so long.

I can't handle it anymore.

My arms reach on their own. One finds her waist, the other cups her neck and I pull her to me.

The first touch of her lips with mine is hard, bruising, and I want more.

Her hands burn into my chest. At first she resists with firm pressure, but as she relents I grip her more tightly.

Sweet acid pours through my limbs, burning me from the inside out. My tongue sweeps over her lips, begging her to let me in.

Coffee and cinnamon is the first thing I taste when she opens and I get her tentative submission.

Her moan grabs my cock with its sultry tone and nearly has me coming in my shorts.

Fiery traces of her fingers move over my chest and she weaves them behind my neck, beckoning me closer with an insistent tug.

My hand buries itself in the blissful gap at the small of her back that has been tantalizing me all morning.

Breathlessly, my lips leave hers and follow a trail down the line of her jaw to the soft hollow beneath her ear.

"I would have married you the day you turned eighteen." My hot breath reflects back the words I push into her between each nibble of her tender skin. "By nineteen, you'd have had our first baby. Maybe two." The stiffness of my cock is no longer a secret as I press it against her flat belly. "By now, the world could burn because we would be filling our corner of it."

Her small gasp is smothered by her teeth nipping on the lobe of my ear.

"Things would have been very different. I'd have taken care of you." My chest presses against her soft breasts that are crying out for me to knead them with my palms.

"You would have?" Her breathy words tickle through the short hairs on my neck as her nails claw into my back, clinging to me.

"Mmhmm." The growl erupts from the depths of my chest. "You've loved me quietly for a decade. I have some catching up to do."

Cupping her ass, I lift her easily to let her legs encircle my waist. The squeal she looses turns into a giggle when I perch her on the wooden bench behind her.

I love how stretchy her tank top is. The teal gives way to reveal the lacy white bra hidden beneath it. A tanned line sits just under the edge, like a beacon drawing my mouth. I find myself tracing the pale line with the tip of my tongue as my hands work their way to the back of the restrictive garment.

Victory is mine as the milky white mounds push out at me, teasing me with their deep pink nipples.

"And, how—" She's interrupted by my teeth biting down on one of her rigid peaks. "Oh, God." Her hands flatten around my head. " How would you catch up?" It's a full, panting breath between each word.

These clothes have to go. I lean back enough to peel them off of her, showing me her bare beauty. I'm enraptured. My own shirt follows hers. Before they've settled on the floor, I have her pulled back against me, my fingers knotting in her hair and tilting her chin up so I can look her in the eyes.

"I'll have to love you fiercely." Plunging my tongue between her lips, I stop any reply she may have.

These last few weeks, I have gotten to know her better than anyone else. Evenings of laughter, beers on the deck, even commiserating over our mutual disgust at Jessica.

I've been happier at the end of the world than any other time in my life.

Her hands leave a burning path as her mouth battles with mine. She works her hips forward so she balances precariously on the edge of the bench.

I do what any gentleman would in my position, I prop her up with my cock. Her damp heat soaks through the thin fabric of my nylon shorts.

She rocks against me making me so hard I'm leaking with the friction.

The need to be inside of her is torturous. I want to pierce her and parade her around while she rides me.

Better than the Nobel Prize.

Fuck science. I have Sarah.

Pushing my palm between us and twisting at the button on her denim shorts, opens them to my exploring fingers.

Molten gold. Her pussy is already soaked. When I stroke lightly over her swollen clit she nearly jerks herself off the lip.

"You're so wet for me, baby. I want to taste you." The last thing I want to do is pull away from between her silky thighs, but it's the only way I can free her from the snug cut-off jeans.

"Caleb, I—" The change in her tone makes me pause, just as the top of her trimmed pussy is coming into view.

Her touch trembles on my arms.

"Hmm?" My response is guttural. Every sense is focused on the apex of her thighs as I drag the last of her clothes off.

"—I never imagined my first time happening in a barn." She's almost whispering.

With so little blood in my brain, it takes me a moment to register what she's telling me.

A surge of fire floods through my body. Every limb tingles and I nearly spurt into my boxers. "I'm your first?"

That devious lip of hers rolls between the white flash of her teeth as she gives me a shy nod. "It was always going to be you."

"Marry me." I didn't intend to say that. But, it's out there. I'll own it.

"What?" Her eyebrows fly up and her pupils grow in the dim light as she stares at me. "You can't be serious."

"I am. With your cherry, I thee wed. I can't imagine any greater proof of commitment than you waiting years for me." My mouth presses over hers before I work my way down her body.

"Don't you think that's, um, hasty?" Her arms brace behind her as she leans back, letting me spread her knees apart as I descend to the shrine of her magnificent, pure, pussy.

The gasp that escapes her pink lips when my tongue touches her clit for the first time sends a shiver into my nuts that makes me reach down and pinch the tip of my dick to keep myself from coming.

This fucking woman. She's juicy and sweet like a ripe nectarine. I want to smother myself in her.

With my cock under control, I gently push my index finger into the vice of her virgin cunt.

Mine.

She moans and her hips twitch as her ankles press against my shoulders.

I can barely move within her, she's so tight. With long slow strokes, I thrust deeper and roll my knuckle to try and loosen the chokehold she has on my hand.

Her cries get shorter as I increase the tempo. One of her hands flies up and pushes on the back of my head, burying my nose against her.

Groaning my approval against the hard little bud of her clit, I slide in a second finger and watch her arch into a silent scream as she spasms in release. Her pussy clamps down so hard I can't move my fingers. I'm trapped within her orgasm, and there's no place else in this entire world I'd rather be.

I can't wait to be in her. I'm going to flood her. She's going to drown from the inside.

But, she's not ready. I don't want to hurt her, despite the fact that my balls feel like they're rupturing watching her.

"That's my good little wifey coming on my face. I'm going to make you do that again to get ready for me." A shudder ripples through her as I roll my fingers.

"Just a, just a sec. I need a—" Her head lolls back as my mouth latches on to her sensitive clit again.

Rolling her between my teeth, I work up a faster pace as she grinds herself against my face. Her thighs quiver along my head.

She's so close. Fuck, so am I. But, I won't ruin this for her.

Her heels dig into my shoulder blades and her ass hovers in the air as her body tightens for a second climax.

"Ah! Caleb!" Sarah screams my name as she writhes on the table top. The muscles in her tight little cunt contract and milk my fingers in a harrowing grip that feels like she's almost cutting off the circulation.

"I want you to always say my name like that. Or 'husband'." I stretch my hand over her lower belly as I taste her again. She's going to be so full, she'll swell with my seed. Then, with my baby.

Ugh, I almost come picturing it.

Those rapid little pants tell me she's getting closer. My girl likes to get off.

And, now I get to join her.

The mewling noises she makes as she squirms grow more frantic as I flatten my tongue against her for one more taste.

Dropping my shorts, my eager cock bobs with readiness. Her knees fall from my shoulders and wrap around my ribs as I work my mouth up her sweaty body. One more hard suction on a reddened nipple before I pull her lips to mine in a feverish kiss.

I can feel her pussy, hot and wet against the mushroomed head of my raging cock. "Baby, I'm gonna go as slow as I can. You're so fucking tight, I don't know how long I'll last. But, I promise, after this time, I'm going to make you come on my cock, and it will be the most amazing thing you've ever felt."

My hips roll gently in short movements as my engorged tip nestles into her scalding hollow. The bite of her nails on my back lessens as her body stretches around me.

"You're doing so good. Breathe, baby. It'll only hurt for a second." Her breasts press against my chest as she takes a long inhale. Warm cinnamon flares over my neck when I cradle her.

Tiny thrusts. My legs shake and my nuts are screaming for release, but I'm gaining with each push. It's a battle of control when every fiber in my body wants to drive into her.

Her moan reinvigorates my resolve. If I wasn't bracing us both on this damn bench, I'd be able to reach down and help bring her to another climax before I bury myself too deep.

Resistance halts me with a firm pressure that makes her muscles squeeze my shaft.

"Ready?" Fuck I'm so close my voice cracks. I barely feel the nod against my jaw before my ass clenches and I ram into her, breaking through the gift she's carried for years just for me.

I can't stop now. Long strokes build in ferocity. Her back arches and tears slick her cheeks. But, her initial gasp of pain transforms into a panting cry as she tugs me into her. The ridge of my cock pushes against her tensing walls as she stiffens beneath me. Her hips rise to meet mine and our bellies slap in a rapid beat of passion until she throws her head back.

And screams my name.

Her cunt locks me down so hard I can't move. My own release comes violently. I'm a prisoner in her divine womb as she strips me of burning ribbons of cum.

My legs threaten to give out on me as aftershocks of her orgasm send pulsating spasms along my length.

Peppering light kisses along the rapid pulse in her throat, I let my softening dick escape. "Thank you. I hope it didn't hurt too badly."

"It felt so much better than I ever expected." Her breathy words tickle down my bare chest.

Still holding her, I push up against the worn wood bench so she's sitting up. Her quivering legs are still wrapped around my waist. I want to keep them there forever.

"It shouldn't hurt next time. I think maybe a nice warm bath will feel good?" I hate stepping out of her warm embrace, but I need to reach our discarded clothes strewn across the floor.

"That does sound nice." A brilliant red blush works up from her chest and up her slender neck. "Next time?" She sounds almost timid in her question.

Sliding her shorts up her tanned legs, I pause at her knees. A tinge stains her thighs and I bury my hand between them. My fingers are darkened with blood and I show them to her. "Yes, next time. And, the time after, again and again. This is proof that you're mine."

Blushing, she gives me a small smile that makes me want to rut into her again.

As she pulls her tank top on, I toss my own shirt and her bra over my shoulder. Before she can protest, I loop my arms under her knees and shoulders and pick her up.

Cradling her, we burst into the heat of the midday sun from the dim barn.

"I can walk." She pats my bare chest.

"I'm carrying my bride over the threshold." Pressing my lips against her temple, she giggles as the screen door slaps behind us.

"What's wrong? Are you hurt?" Levi jumps from the couch when he sees us.

Her flaming skin burns against me. "I'm fine."

His brows furrow. "I don't get it. Where are you going?" He follows me down the hall to the big bathroom door.

"I'm going to give my wife a warm bath." I can't fight the grin.

Sarah gasps and giggles.

Her brother looks at us open mouthed. "Huh?"

"You heard him." Her laughter nearly overtakes her words. "My husband is going to give me a bath."

Jesus. I'm hard again.

Chapter 10

Jessica

Finally. I get to leave this rotten cabin.

It's been weeks. Most of my friends are ignoring me. My life is ruined being stuck here in the woods like some sort of hillbilly.

I've even let some of my clothes wrinkle as they've gone into my bags. Using the dry cleaner's app, I've already made an appointment for them to come and pick up all of my outfits for decontamination.

They're infested with poor. It needs purged.

Maybe I should just burn them. Isn't that what people used to do?

I'm sure it's a thing.

"Levi! I'm ready!" Where is he? He said today is the day we get the stupid shots and then I can go home.

The wheels on my makeup bag hit every gap in the tiled floor in rhythm with my heels. I want to look on top today. My social media feeds are all filled with my updates about heading home. So, just in case anyone wants to throw me a party, I need to be fabulous.

Ew. Sarah and Caleb are making out in the kitchen. Gag.

It's the grossest that they hooked up. She's such a ho.

Caleb seems like a nice enough guy. Why he would want to end up with someone as mean as her doesn't make any sense.

Whatever. I'm so gone.

"Levi!" The front door is open with only the screen in place. What is he doing?

Careful of the fresh polish on my nails, I push through the flimsy door to the porch. "You look like you're giving his car a blowjob."

He pulls the tube from his mouth and dumps the end into a red gas can. "It's a long drive to the vet clinic, Jess. We need the gas to get there and back. I don't know if the stations will be open."

Trickling fluid sounds echo from the container at his feet and a haze of shimmering air floats above the spigot.

"It stinks. I have on Dior. You're going to ruin it with that yuck." Sliding the handle to my case down into its sheath, I'll just leave this right here so he can put it in our SUV for me.

His groan follows me as I turn away. "Maybe I should just spray this on you? One little spark from your bitchy personality, and none of us will have to worry about what you smell like."

I can hear him laughing to himself.

Asshole.

The fact that I have to roll my luggage to the front door by myself makes me even more mad at him. What an awful husband. He's supposed to take care of me.

This has not worked out for me. When I get back, I'm calling Daddy to help me get a divorce.

"What are you doing?" Sarah stops me on my third trip.

"What does it look like, Sarah?" God, she can be so dumb.

Her hands cross over her breasts. They're smaller than mine, but I bought and paid for them. The best twenty thousand I've ever spent. She should invest in her chest, she'd get a better man.

"We aren't going there today, Jess. The vet clinic is in the opposite direction." The bitch has the audacity to smile.

Rage builds in me. No, I'm keeping my cool. That was the deal.

A finger up to her to make my point. "Levi said, I get the shot, I get to go home. All together." I will *not* let Raggedy Anne see me cry.

The chemical burn singes my nose before Levi steps onto the porch and pulls the screen. "I'll take you home tomorrow, Jess. It's already going to be five hours in the car today. So put your shit back in the room and we'll go in the morning. We need the space in the car for supplies if we can find any stores open." He pushes between us to go to the kitchen.

Tears blur my vision. One nail breaks as I dig them into my palms to try and keep myself from screaming. "You promised." I hate that my voice wavers.

"I said 'after'. I didn't say—" The water in the sink turns on, drowning out the rest of his words.

It's so fucking hard to walk fast in this tight skirt, but I'm positive I make it look epic as I pull my things back to the study.

Slamming the heavy oak door as hard as I can does make me feel a little better.

Just one more step. Tomorrow. I'll be back.

Shit. Now I need to update my status so everyone knows when to show up.

It's so strange that my earlier ones hardly have any likes or views. Why are they all ghosting me?

Oh my god, my mascara is running. Stop sniveling! It doesn't work anymore.

Tossing my shoulders back, I strut through the house and crawl directly into the passenger seat. If this is what it takes, let's get it over with.

Sarah and Caleb sit in the back seat. Her annoying giggles make me want to vomit.

Levi keeps grinding his teeth when he looks at me. He disgusts me too.

After almost an hour, the bumpy dirt road smooths onto the pavement. As the first buildings start to pass by, I feel like a load has been lifted.

Civilization.

Well, a puny, worn down version of it.

"Check out the cars." Caleb leans between the front seats and gestures toward the side of the road.

Several have their hoods crumpled with smears of dark reddish-brown.

They look tacky.

"I don't see anyone. Do you think they're all infected?" Sarah's voice drifts from the back.

She can be so ridiculous.

"Just look at this town. I bet they're so broke they don't even have running water. Diseases run rampant in hovels." It won't be like this in Beverly Hills. That's where it will be safe to go.

I can't wait to get back with normal people.

Levi's squeezes the steering wheel and his jaw muscle starbursts along the side of his face. "This is everywhere, Jess. But, I guess you'll find out tomorrow."

Yes. One more day until freedom.

The disgusting drudgery of the village fades as we climb into a series of increasing hills. A resort sits near the top.

"I need to stop." My bladder is painfully full.

"It's only another hour." Levi stares straight ahead as he answers.

Sarah squirms in the backseat and lets loose another low giggle before her hand grabs my seat and she pulls herself closer. "I could stop, too."

Of course she wants to be like me.

"Fine," Levi grumbles as he turns us into the large parking lot.

It has a mountain lodge vibe. Very bougie, but it's trending. I need to get a selfie for my followers.

"Sarah, take my picture." My phone dangles by the pop socket in my fingers as I hold it out to her. "My stick is in my bag. Be sure to be lower than me, and don't take it until I say."

She raises one of her natural eyebrows. Who has those anymore?

"No." The bitch keeps walking.

"We're coming with you." Caleb unfolds from the back seat and catches up quickly.

Levi saunters, letting the space between us grow with every step. I bet he's enjoying the view of me walking in front of him.

High beams and a huge foyer welcome us as we step through the heavy glass doors.

Huh. Weird, the lights are off. That must be where all the help is, fixing them.

I don't need a concierge to show me where the restroom is. There's a sign indicating they're just past the lobby. Without pausing, I flip the flashlight on my cell to illuminate the dim hall.

They really should have someone set up temporary lighting. This is unacceptable.

I'm going to post a review of their poor service.

Sarah's footsteps are quieter in her sneakers. God, she even sounds like a peasant.

My hand flattens against the brass push plate.

"Let me check it out first." Caleb puts his hand on the door near mine.

"Ew. Gross. You don't need to go in like some creeper, Caleb. It's fine." Ducking under his arm, Sarah follows closely before leaving him standing in the hall.

His deep voice is muffled by the oak. "Yell if you need me."

I rarely use the first stall, but I'm dying. Sarah clicks the lock on the third one down.

"I think the plumbing is backing up." She complains so much.

Ignoring her feels so good. They do it to me all of the time.

"I'm serious. There's sticky shit on the floor back here and it's not flushing." She's so loud banging around in there.

"Do you have to make so much noise? I can't pee with all of your whining and crashing around, Sarah." My review of this place is really going to be bad. There's barely enough toilet paper for me to wipe.

"I'm not banging. I think there's—" Sarah is cut off by a scratching sound followed by a low moan.

That's it. I'm sick of her. Flinging the door open, I step out of the stall as she unlocks hers.

Shadows from my phone's light flicker across her face revealing surprise when I push her backwards.

"I hate all of you! You lie to me, treat me like garbage, act like you're better than me! You're nothing!"

I can't make a fist, I might break a nail.

"Jesus Christ, Jessica! What the fuck is wrong with you?" Her cell clatters across the floor as I swing my arm at her again.

A dark figure steps from one of the back stalls and stumbles towards us.

She can wait her turn.

"You can't even be quiet when I ask!" My vision has tinges of red at the edges. I'm so angry, I could claw her eyes out. "I'm so sick of your psycho family!"

One more hard shove and she flies backwards against the mystery woman.

Let her deal with that.

When she screams, Caleb rushes past me, his phone a narrow beam of light blazing through.

I never want to come back to this hotel. One star. Would not recommend.

They're all pissed at me, but that's nothing new. I guess the crazy lady in the bathroom scratched Sarah in the tousle and they all think it's my fault.

Eighteen more hours.

My arm itches where I got the vaccine from the ancient veterinarian, but at least that hurdle is done.

No one talks to me. I guess she finally listened about shutting up and leaving me alone.

Since it's obvious that Levi isn't going to help me, I'm loading the SUV by myself with all of my stuff.

Look at me, I'm a strong, independent woman. I don't need him. Or, any of them.

A piercing shriek echoes through the house, followed by loud sobbing.

She's so obnoxious.

Levi runs up the steps two at a time while I roll my last bag down the hall to the front door.

The screen bounces as it closes behind me and I let my luggage drop down the three stairs to the concrete walk.

It's as I'm struggling to lift it into the back of the Land Rover that Levi reappears.

His face is so red it makes his eyes look like they're glowing blue balls in the fading sunlight.

"You pushed her into that woman?" His head drops to almost level with mine.

"She was being a bitch." I should have done more.

I don't see his hand move until it hits me.

Pain explodes across my lips and nose in a fiery burst.

My ears ring and tears spring to blur the world.

I think he busted my—

Another fist hits my cheek. The crunch of the bone rattles into my skull as my jaws snap against each other.

"Please! No!" Trying to throw my hands up, they're stopped with his arm as another lightning storm erupts behind my eyes when he strikes me again.

It knocks me off my feet. Gravel bites into my elbows and hip. The thin skirt offers no protection against the jagged edges of the stones.

"You're the fucking bitch." Spittle flies from his mouth that sprays across my chest. "She got bit because of you. She's going to die because of you." He hand wraps around my throat and squeezes, lifting my shoulders off of the ground.

Another blow leaves stars in my sight and hard crunchy things in my mouth.

My god. I think those are my teeth.

I can't breathe. Kicking out my legs does little except scrape them even worse. Every perfect nail breaks as I try to pull at his fingers and scratch at his wrist.

But, he holds tight until I'm too weak to fight back.

My heavy arms fall useless by my sides. It's only then he loosens enough for me to take a gulping breath.

His hand moves from my neck to grabbing a handful of my hair.

Needles stab into my scalp as he begins dragging me.

Why can't I move? Everything feels so heavy and dull. Each time I breathe, it's like I'm having to force air through a straw.

A stick rakes down my leg and the smell of rotting leaves covers me as he tugs me into the woods.

Is he going to kill me? I don't deserve this.

All I did was a little push. Is it really my fault Sarah is a clumsy ho who can't keep her balance?

He dumps me unceremoniously into the damp dirt. Stars still float in my sight as his nails tear into my blouse.

My weighted arms get lifted together.

What is he doing? I can't move my hands apart. Something tight is around them.

Am I tied?

With a nauseating swing, I'm held up by whatever binding is around my wrists until I'm hugging the rough bark of a tree.

"Please, no." My lips are so fat it's hard to talk through them. The burning pain radiates down into my bruised throat.

Just my tiptoes brush against the root beneath me.

Where are my shoes?

"I should have done this a long time ago." His voice is hoarse, but doesn't cover the jangle of his belt buckle.

"Levi! Baby, I'm sorry."

There's a low whirring sound before the thudding bite of the buckle hitting me in the small of the back.

I can't stop the scream that tears out of my tender mouth.

"You wanted to be a brat, I should have put you in your place." His grunt covers the sound of his belt cutting through the air.

The prod of his buckle embeds itself near my spine when it hits before the weight pulls it away.

He hits me again and again.

All I can do is scream until one of my ribs crack with his ferocious strike.

Blood runs down my legs. My back, ass, and thighs are covered with the welts of each stroke.

"This is how you should be." He's panting as he closes in on me. "Fucking broken." Roughly, he pulls down the last of my skirt, leaving me bare to the cold night.

"Open your legs." Hot breath sears across every wound. I can't talk. I can't move.

He kicks my ankles from under me so I'm hanging against the spiky tree, the bark is like sandpaper.

"You know what a good brat is?" He wraps the leather strap of the belt around my swollen neck and knots it into his fist with my hair.

His elbow grinds against my spine as he forces my head to turn left to right, dragging my face against the tree until blood pours from my lips.

"No? A good brat is beaten, fucked, and left for dead."

Still holding the belt so tightly my every breath is a wheeze, his other hand moves between us.

The unmistakable sound of his zipper filters through my pained haze.

Trying to pinch my legs together is pointless as I feel how hard he is pressing on me. He pushes the engorged head of his cock against my asshole and nausea swirls in my stomach. I've never let him do that to me.

When he thrusts into me, it feels like I'm tearing in half. A new cry pushes past the strangling twist of the belt as he pulls back and forces himself in again, further.

Warm and wet runs down my thighs as a new level of agony ignites within me.

His fingers bruise into my hip as he pulls my body onto his pistoning cock. Every time he rams me, it's a hot fire poker burning its way deeper inside.

The tether on my throat tightens, forcing my head back until his lips are touching my ear. "You're a worthless whore." He spasms his release, acidic jets that sting long after he pulls out.

His hand and the belt disappear. Taking a full lungful of air sends a stabbing catch into my chest as my rib pops and flexes.

Something heavy hits me in the back of the head, bouncing my nose on the hard surface of the tree before everything goes black.

It's the shivering that wakes me. Then, it's the pain.

Dawn washes through the forest with the misty dew rising like steam around me.

My legs don't want to work, aching in protest as I try and gain footing. When I manage to work my arms off of the low branch he had me hanging from, they fall like lead and tumble me to the ground. They're completely numb.

Pins and needles soon follow, but at least they work. And are the least damaged of my tortured body.

He treated me like an animal, dragging me into the woods.

It takes forever to tear the torn remains of my shirt from around my wrists. My mouth hurts too much to even open, but after several minutes of twisting, I manage to get loose.

Everything hurts so much. I can barely see out of one eye, my nose is so swollen I can't breathe through it.

Today is freedom day.

Falling several times on my twisted path back to the house, I make it to Caleb's Jeep for support.

I nearly trip again over the gas can that Levi left.

It still has some fuel in it, but it's light enough I can carry it.

Careful to not make any noise going into the house, I find the two things in the kitchen I need.

A knife and matches.

There's enough gasoline to cover the couch and leave a trail to the porch. I can't even smell it, but the chemical burns my throat.

It takes me three tries to get a flame.

The rapid whoosh of the fire pushes me back and I lose my precarious balance.

Fresh blood pools out of me on the gravel. I don't even know which injury it's coming from. Right now, I don't even care.

One last thing.

Slashing tires is harder than I thought it would be. It is so hard to get the knife to go through the thick rubber. But, once I figure it out, the rest are easier.

I hope Levi didn't disable the Land Rover when we got back since we were going to leave this morning.

Naked and shaking, I crawl into the driver's seat. When the engine purrs to life, it feels better than winning the lottery.

Chapter 11

Sarah

I feel hot. Pushing away from Caleb's sleeping body, a wave of acrid heat flows between us.

Is that smoke?

"Caleb! Wake up!" He rouses quickly, sleep still heavy on his face.

"Are you okay?" The worry that plagued his features yesterday returns.

"I'm fine, but I think there's a fire!" I turn away and fling the clinging covers off of me. Every limb feels heavy and sore, but adrenaline fuels my movements.

He rolls out the other side and tugs his shorts up. "Shit, I gotta grab my laptop, it has my research on it!" With his shoes in his hand, he pulls the door open to a billow of dark smoke pluming across the ceiling. "Sarah! Get out now!" He bolts down the hall as he yells.

Fuck. My head aches as I try to focus on what I need to grab. Luckily, my backpack is nearby. Computer, phone, change of clothes, car keys. That will have to do it.

The air is getting heavy and burns my lungs with every breath. Caleb meets me in the hall and grabs my hand, tugging me toward the stairs.

Flames have engulfed the living room and are creeping up the walls. My skin feels like it's scalding as we dart past to the kitchen and push out through the screen door.

The cold night air is a soothing relief on my body, but doesn't dampen the fear for my brother when I don't see him.

"Levi!" I scream as loud as I can, hoping he can hear me and is outside. Back into the kitchen so I'm closer, the stinging heat scorches my eyes. "Levi!"

Caleb grabs my elbow and pulls me back outside.

"You can't go back in there! He's probably already out. Let's check around the house. I'll go look in the barn real quick." He pauses, staring at me in the flickering light. "Don't go back in, Sarah."

"I need to make sure." Popping sounds come from the growing fire. I can see the kitchen is being overtaken and the stairs are hidden by the raging inferno.

If Levi is still in there, he won't have long.

"Fuck. Sarah, no! Let's go around and check the study. I don't remember hearing him on the stairs." He drags me off the porch, his grip a vise on my arm.

He's running so fast, I almost stumble trying to keep up. My legs feel sluggish as I force them to make every hurried step.

Caleb reaches the window, his scowl illuminated by the blaze. "Shit, get back. He's in there." Freeing me from his grasp, he picks up a heavy rock and throws it through the glass. "Levi! Get up!"

I manage to get a glimpse over his shoulder as he pushes the broken shards inward.

Levi is sprawled on the floor with an empty liquor bottle still clutched in his hand.

Did he get drunk last night?

Was it because of me? He was torn up when I told him about the bite. I haven't seen him so struck with grief since our parents died.

"Levi!" Caleb's deep voice carries over the roaring of the fire. "Wake up, man!" He tries to wedge himself through the narrow metal frame of the window, but falls back. He's too big.

The study door is turning black with the ghosting of cinders beginning to appear.

"Lift me in." My fingers knot in Caleb's shirt. "I can drag him over. I know he'll fit through." I can't just stand here.

"No, Sarah. He's too heavy. You'll both die." His dark eyes shimmer with tears.

I thought we both cried ourselves empty last night.

"I'm already dead, Caleb." Reality is setting in. The bite on my leg is a death sentence. "At least let me try to save him first."

He squeezes his eyes shut and shoves his fists against his temples. "I'm not ready to lose you! I just got you."

My hands find his wrists as I press myself against him. "Please? At least this is a better death than losing myself like those mindless beasts." A shiver runs down my spine at the memory of the empty stare of the woman as she clawed at me. The caked blood around her mouth and down the front of her throat. I can almost smell the rot again when her fetid breath washed over me.

His palms wrap around my cheeks as he pulls me in for a bruising kiss. "I won't let you die. I promise you. But, I can't save you if you get trapped in there." His fingers curl behind my neck to touch his lips gently against my forehead. "Come back to me if you can't move him."

I can't talk past the lump in my throat, but I nod against him.

In a blur, he has me turn and lifted so I can start wiggling my way carefully past the jagged glass.

Just in time to see a tongue of fire shoot across the carpet and take hold of the puddle of spilled bourbon. It rockets into knee-high flames when it touches Levi's pants.

He wakes up screaming.

The sound is so heart-wrenching, I don't get my arms up in time and fall against the shards scattered on the floor. Blood pours across my vision, but I manage to push myself to my feet and run over to him.

"Levi! Stop moving!" I'm trying to pat the embers out as he writhes.

Red, welted flesh erupts through the scorched fabric. My hand sticks to him when I smack it.

Finally extinguished, he throws himself flat, his back arching off the floor. "It hurts, it hurts so bad."

"I know, but you have to get up!" I manage to grab a hold of one of his flailing arms and pull him a few inches before he jerks himself free.

"No! God, no! It fucking hurts! Leave me." Throwing his arm over his face, he gestures violently at me, waving me away.

"We aren't both dying. Just please, for me." My grasp slips wrestling with him, but I pull him another foot closer to Caleb.

"You need to hurry, Sarah." Caleb reaches his arm through, beckoning me.

"Levi, help me. Push with your feet." He's so heavy. And, my legs just aren't as strong.

Soot riddles the wounds on his legs and the putrid smell of burnt flesh mixes with the polluted air to make my stomach twist.

One of his weeping knees rises and he digs it into the charred carpet to help with my momentum.

"That's it, just a little more." Caleb strains his fingers and brushes my shoulder.

I'm so close.

My legs shake with the effort, my lungs burn in search of oxygen, but I get one more good tug and he's close enough for Caleb to wrap around Levi's wrist.

A groan escapes my brother as Caleb pulls him up the wall.

"Pull his waist out so I'm not dragging him over the sill," Caleb grunts as he heaves Levi's arms through the narrow window.

I can barely breathe. Wheezing, I pull his hips back and do my best to lift as much as possible.

Weakness overtakes me and I lose my grip.

Levi screams as his ribs rake over the glass. Blood drips down the wall with every movement of his mangled body.

Tears muddy my sight. I did that to him. My own shortcomings.

With renewed strength, I save his hips from being ravaged by the broken window fragments.

Sobs wrack me as his feet disappear.

"Come on. Give me your hands." Caleb reaches bloody hands out to me.

Is it his, or Levi's? Is it my fault?

My trembling arms seek his, and I'm vaulted to the narrow gap. Twisting my body, he picks me up gingerly so I don't drag on the cutting edge.

Wrapping me against him, his face presses against the top of my head. "You did it. You're amazing."

The comfort of his touch almost covers the tragedy unfolding around us.

Another pop from the inferno snaps us out of the moment and we both rush to Levi.

"Grab his other arm." Caleb hoists Levi up and we carry him away from the engulfed house towards the cars.

Where is the Land Rover?

Guilt overtakes me. I never once thought about Jessica.

She must have taken it. Did she start the fire? Levi was mad when I told him she had pushed me into the woman who bit me.

What happened after that, I have no idea. Caleb and I stayed up late mourning the life we'll never have together.

"Let's take him to the jeep." He's holding almost all of Levi's weight, and I still feel overwhelmed.

The stress of yesterday and now the house are taking its toll on me.

I don't remember Caleb's car sitting so low.

"Fuck." The word is low, almost under his breath, but realization hits like a sledgehammer.

All of the tires are flat.

Crap, so are mine on my Subaru.

That bitch.

"Sarah, I'll hold him up. I think there's a clean blanket in my rig. Can you spread it on the grass for him?" Caleb leans with Levi so I can unwind myself from my brother.

When Levi is down, all he does is moan.

He needs a doctor.

Dialing an ambulance just lands me on a busy signal. Police and fire is the same.

Shit.

"Sarah, I'm sorry," Levi mumbles between his groans. "She burned our house down because of me."

"This wasn't your fault." I try to kneel slowly next to him, but my legs give out and a fall in a crumple at his side.

His hand finds mine and he grips me tightly. "I married her. It is my fault."

"Okay, yea. You win that one." I try to give him a small smile. My head hurts so much.

Something trickles down the side of my face. Blood, from when I fell.

"I'm going to get as much out of the barn as I can in case it catches." Caleb's warm palm rests on my shoulder before he disappears into the darkness.

Levi's fingers go limp.

"No, no, no. Levi?" Hugging against him, I put my ear over his heart.

A gentle beat thrums within his chest. He's just unconscious.

Closing my eyes, I focus on the rhythm .

How did I get here? The last time I was in San Antonio I was only sixteen. The unmistakable heat is filled with the sounds and smells of the Boardwalk. Lights on strings weave over the canal with all of the shops and restaurants nestled shoulder to shoulder along the edges.

There's the place I bought my favorite bracelet. I wore it until I was in college and it broke all over the cafeteria floor.

My best friend Sammy? Oh my god! I haven't seen her since I graduated! She is so young.

"Sarah! Where have you been? Aren't you going to meet us for lunch?" Her blonde hair bounces around her face as she excitedly shifts on her toes. "Mark Connell is going to be there!" Her blue eyes widen before she gives me an exaggerated wink.

It doesn't hold the same weight now. Mark always reminded me of Caleb, maybe that's why I thought I had a crush on him, too.

"Besides, that place has the best food in Texas. Aren't you hungry?" She pulls on my arm, turning me to face one of the bright bulbs hovering overhead.

It hurts my head to look at it.

"Yea, I guess I could eat." My stomach growls. When was my last meal? It seems like ages ago.

"Here, have a seat." She pulls a padded chair from the long table filled with my friends from high school.

They're all here. It's like a reunion in time. How? I don't even remember all their names, but the faces look so familiar.

The smell of fresh barbeque makes my insides knot in hunger. I'm ravenous.

A thin waiter with a broad hat smiles beneath his wide waxed mustache as he sets plates of ribs and brisket before us.

It all looks so delicious.

"Here, I know this one is your favorite." Sammy gives me a light giggle as she hands me a long beef rib dripping with *sauce. It's so tender it's sagging off the bone as she slides it onto my plate.*

"Aren't you eating?" No one else has food, they're all watching me.

My hands shake with eagerness. I've felt so weak, surely this will give me the energy I need.

"This one is for you. You'll love it, I'm sure." Her bright white smile doesn't quite reach the sapphires of her eyes.

The huge chunk of meat drips down my hand off my elbows, but I can't resist. When my teeth tear into the first bite, it melts into my mouth in a flavor explosion. Sweet, a little salty, and cooked to perfection. Raw. Just how I like it.

"Sarah? What are you doing?" Sammy asks with a flip of her hair.

I can't answer, the beef is a new form of heaven sliding into me.

"Sarah! What are you doing?" Caleb grabs my shoulder as the restaurant disappears.

"What do you mean?" I must have been dreaming.

My hands are still touching the heat of the saucy meat.

What? The barbecue smell fades into one of soot and ash.

Looking down, Levi's stomach is bared open, my fingers knotted in the ropes of his intestines. A pool of blood spreads beneath my knees.

"No! Oh God! What have I done?" My ear finds his chest.

Silence.

Chapter 12

Peter

A god deserves a throne.

Or, at least a castle. Like the ones in Beverly Hills. I don't think anyone can stop me if they wanted to.

No police, no military. Hell, I haven't even seen any signs of the gangs that used to loiter the streets of L.A. Chicken shits.

Someone needs to lead the mortals. Who better than me?

I don't recognize the name of the celebrity that hangs on the wrought iron gate, but it doesn't matter. This mansion is the only place that is fitting for me.

The solar panels and functioning fountain are what I'm more interested in. That, and the eight foot concrete wall that surrounds my new kingdom. A complete playground is a bonus.

It makes my cock hard thinking of all the ways I could use the equipment once I have more girls.

Getting in to the main door was easier than I thought. It wasn't locked.

"Hello, honey! I'm home!" Well, isn't this quaint? A whole extended banister I could tie a slut off of every post.

It's no surprise when silence answers me. But, I still better check everything out. I don't want any unexpected guests.

What's this? A bone. It looks like it's from a leg. Right about the same size as mine, and I'm not a small man.

The heft on it is about the same as a crow bar, with a nice knob at the end. Whoever left it did me the favor of cleaning it for me.

Where there's smoke, there's fire. Where is the mouth that left this?

"Come out, come out, wherever you are." My yell echoes through the grand ceilings with crown molding bouncing it back to me.

My bone club makes a satisfying thump against each door before I push them open. A study, a bathroom, and a library all greet me one at a time.

When I get nearer to the kitchen, I hear what I've been waiting on.

Scrabbling near the back. "Little mouse, show yourself." The granite counter resonates like a drum when I bounce the fat end of my makeshift mace off of it.

A brief glimpse of a dark and greasy head rises, but never crests the far edge of the island.

Stepping closer, I see the dried blood first. Then, another cleaned bone. A pelvis. Ribs.

It's a child bent over the last of the defleshed corpse. I can't tell if it's a girl or a boy with the wild hair that hangs past its ears. The long strands clinging to the skull in its lap would indicate a woman though.

"Well, mommy fed you one last time?" I kinda want to see what the tiny heathen will do as I stand here. "Decide your fate, kid."

Glassy eyes glance up at me before it stuffs its small hand back through the eye socket. Pulling out a putrid handful of mush, it licks its stained fingers.

"You're a nasty little shit, aren't you? I don't really have time for a fucking Chucky doll running around." It only takes one solid strike with my handy new toy to bash its little noggin it.

The skeleton is easy to walk over so I can check the door behind it. A pantry. Fully loaded. "Hot damn. All this food, kid. And you went for head instead."

That's funny. I could go for some head right now, too. A long blowjob from a seasoned whore would be perfect. What would be the odds I could find myself a good old fashioned virgin I could gag with my dick.

I like that idea. There's enough food here for half the city. What kind of soiree could I throw to bring me some pussy? This place has all the necessities and more.

But, I'm absolutely not taking care of everything myself. Helpers. Staff. Hell, servants. That's what I need.

I'll offer safety in exchange for labor. The few survivors I've crossed paths with would suck my cock for the illusion of it. They'd line up on their knees so I can get rid of the mouths.

Looky here. A walk-in freezer. Packed. Prime rib, rack of lamb, there's so much.

God damn.

Dropping my zipper, I stroke myself as I wander the frigid room. The cold air feels amazing on my balls as I fuck my own fist. When I spurt all over a case of lobster tails, it seems fitting.

I am gourmet. Top tier.

The apex.

Signs will be a good start. Some advertising to bring some people in.

I need a list of rules, too.

Shit, never thought I'd turn into a fucking secretary in the end of the world.

Number one, I'm in charge. Everyone will have to kiss my ass.

Number two, see rule one.

Easy enough.

I'll figure out the rest later. I got the important ones down.

The rest of the day fades into exploring my new place and making signs.

Haven is a good name. Sounds convincing.

What a beautiful day to found my empire. Baby steps. Five signs hung on the major intersections with directions to find me.

Waiting at the gate is a boring way to pass the morning. But, without anyone else to watch it, I'm stuck here.

"Is this you?" A broad shouldered, narrow headed guy calls up to where I'm laying on the small guard shack.

"Yea. Why the fuck did you tear the sign down?" Dumbass.

His wide features fall.

How did he survive this long?

"If you put it back where you found it, you can come back, okay?" I can't judge on brains. Brawn is handy, too. And he looks like he has lots of it.

"I'm Johnny. I'll be back. Can you save me a place?" He twists the cardboard in his hands.

Jesus. "Yes, there will be a spot. How would you like to be the guard here at the gate letting people in?" I need a bag of blow-pops for this moron. Maybe a sticker.

His smile is creepy big. "That would be nice. What's your name?"

"I'm Peter. You can call me 'boss'." There isn't a hammer big enough to knock smarts through his skull.

Note to self, keep him on my side.

His head drops with his grin, then he turns and trots back the way he came.

By the time he gets back, I've fetched a two-way radio from the house and set him up with it.

Ten minutes of my life showing him how to push the damn red button when he talks, I'll never get back.

Whatever.

By the end of the day, five more people have arrived. I now have a cook, a housekeeper, and a couple more guards.

Too bad they're all dudes.

On the second day, five more guys show up. I need a new rule.

Strolling down to the gate, my thigh bone props on my shoulder. I'm a little partial to it. "Johnny, you only let men in if they bring a woman. I don't give a shit if she's a mouther. She can still be used, okay?"

His comic book flattens against his chest in his haste to stand. "Yes, boss. Got it, boss." He even flings me a crappy salute.

The white stick of a lolly pop extends out of the edge of his mouth. I knew they'd win him over.

Sullivan jogs over to me. He's new as of this morning. But, the gang tats that decorate his ruddy face and neck tell me he's far from naive.

He's my new supply run coordinator.

Look at me, official as fuck.

"How much muscle can I use, boss?" He gestures at the pistol lodged in his belt.

"I don't care. Bring me back whatever you can find. We'll fine tune as we add more people. I'm working on rounding up some entertainment." With a heavy wink, he should know what I'm talking about.

His gaping smile reveals gold caps on the back of his teeth. "Alright, boss! That's what I'm talkin' about." He grabs the crotch of his baggy jeans before jogging away.

They can have my leftovers. I get first dibs.

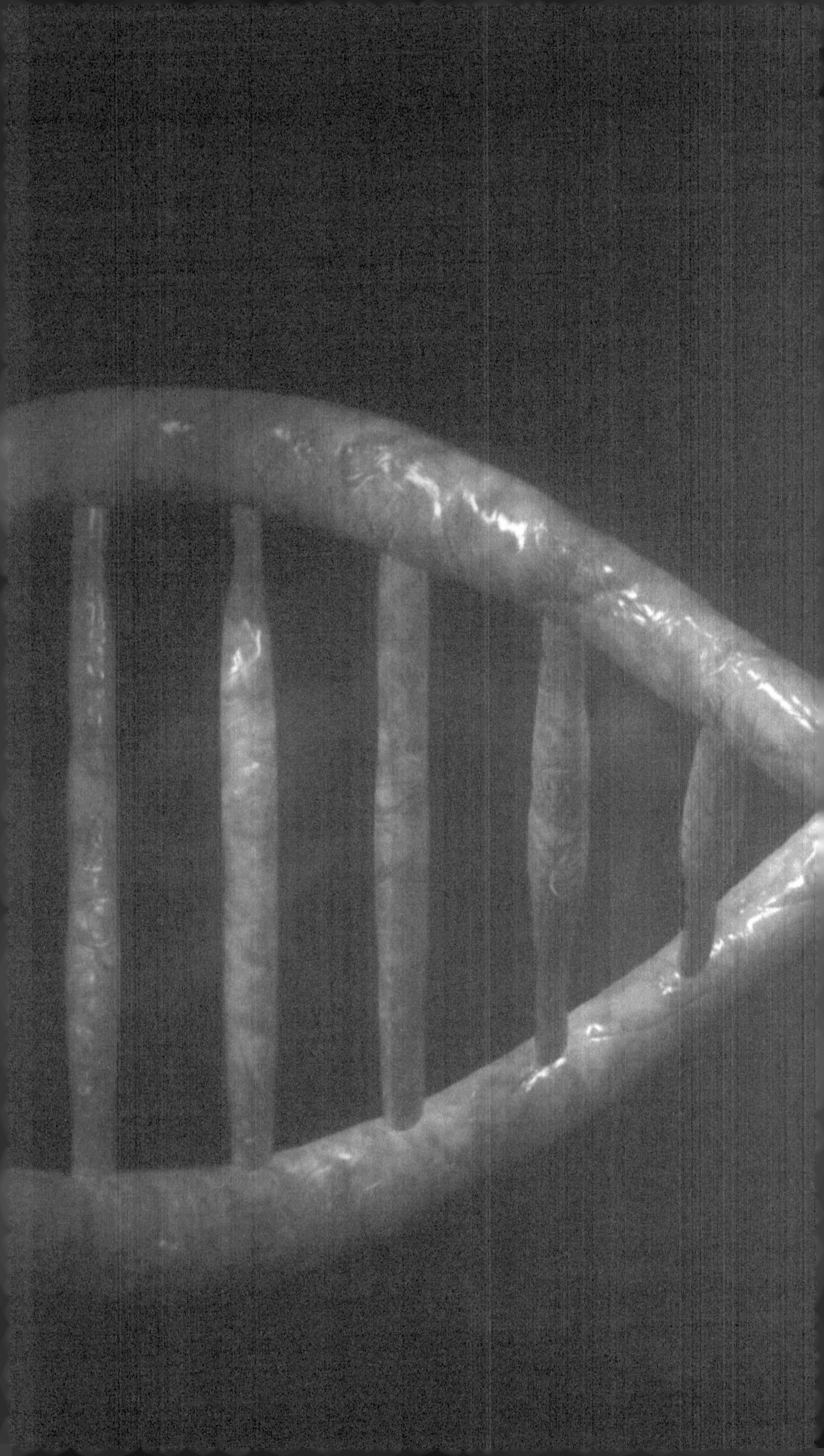

Chapter 13

Caleb

Conflicting emotions rage within me. I swear I'm going to kill Jessica if I ever see her again. Her vapid selfishness is what led to all of this.

Sarah's bite.

The burning house.

Even Levi's death.

They all fall squarely on her narcissistic shoulders.

My joke of burying her in the garden is going to become a reality.

I'd start hunting her down right now, except Sarah needs me. She seems to be having some kind of strange reaction to the illness.

How she managed to slip back to consciousness after succumbing to the hunger, I don't know. All the case studies I've researched say that once they get hungry, they don't turn back. So, it gives me a sliver of hope.

It had to be the vaccine being administered so soon after the bite. That's the only logical thing I can come up with for why she's a crying mess in my arms.

"How could I?" she sobs against my chest. "It's my brother!" Another shuddering wail overtakes her.

Holding her tightly, I stroke my hand down her tangled hair. "It isn't you, baby. The virus is trying to take control. Look how strong you are? You're still talking to me. Do you know how amazing that is?"

Will it last?

My stomach twists at the thought of her turning into one of those mindless eaters. Blindly reaching toward anything that resembles food.

Heated by the dying inferno of our refuge, I rock her slowly as her cries quiet.

What the fuck are we going to do? It's forty miles to town. Can she make it that far? We can't stay here. There wasn't much in the barn except some camping supplies.

At least I have my pistol in my backpack. But, there's very little food.

I need to get her to a lab. I might be able to figure out why she came back.

While we're stretched out in the back of my Jeep, I try and weigh all of the options with the flickering light of the flames bouncing off the windows. Her breathing slows into a steady rhythm as she slips into sleep.

I'm woken by pain digging into my chest.

"Hun-gry." Her voice is guttural against my cheek.

Fuck.

"I'll get you some food, hold on, baby." Scrambling, I know I have a stash of granola bars still in here.

Peeling back the foil wrapper, I hand it to her as her nails continue to rake down my ribs. "Easy, Sarah. That hurts."

Her eyes are foggy, unfocused. It's like she's dreaming. Shit. I don't think she's bounced all the way back.

Crumbs fly as she shoves the snack bar between her teeth. Barely chewing, her fingers grip my shirt as she lets out another rumbling moan. "More."

Six more bars disappear quickly into her flaccid face, devoid of any emotion as she powers through chewing and gulping as fast as she can.

At the seventh one, her fervor slows and her gaze shifts from the window to me. "Caleb?" Her brows crinkle in the center of her forehead. "Why are you looking at me like that?"

"I'm waiting to see if you're going to eat me." I offer her another unwrapped morsel.

This time, she takes it gingerly and holds it in front of her, confusion wrinkling her nose. "I don't understand."

"Neither do I. I've never seen someone exhibit your symptoms. Do you remember waking up?" My touch is soft as I raise each eyelid, checking her emerald irises for their reaction to the growing sunlight.

She doesn't feel warm. Her pulse is normal. If it wasn't for the crumbs on her shirt, I'd have never guessed she was completely disconnected just a few minutes ago.

"No. I was having a dream I was at a birthday party and there was cake." The pink of her tongue darts over her lips. "How many of these did I eat?"

Offering her a lopsided smile and the last two granola bars, still in their wrappers, I shrug. "That one is number eight."

Her chin quivers. The sealed packages crinkle in her hand and she tosses them onto the blanket spread. "I don't remember." Tears tremble in her eyes as they find me. "Please, don't let me hurt you. I can't lose you."

"Sarah, the fact that you're talking to me gives me hope. There might be a way to reverse your symptoms. In the meantime, if all I have to do is keep you fed, that's what a good husband would do. I'll take care of you." Finding her fingers, I intertwine them with my own and bring them to my lips. "I love you. There's no way in hell I'm going to stop fighting for you."

Fat droplets run down her cheeks as she falls into my arms. "I'm so scared. What if I lose control and there's no food? We're trapped out here without any."

My mind races with all of the options. "Let's start with making sure you're full now. And make a plan. I'd really like to get you to a lab. Mine is eighty miles away. If we can find a car, I think we'll be okay."

She sniffs against my shirt and nods without looking up. "There were lots on the way to the veterinarian's. Maybe one of those still has the keys in it."

A cold chill washes over me remembering all the blood stains that marked those vehicles. But, we need to get someplace I can run some tests on her. "I think that's a good idea. We'll pack our bags and start walking."

Gathering what meager supplies I can find doesn't take long.

We're woefully underprepared. But, there's no option to stay here.

"Sarah? Are you ready?" I have the only backpack loaded so she only has to carry a few things.

She's kneeling next to the blanket draped body of Levi. As I get closer I can hear the grisly sound of chewing.

Jesus Christ.

"Sarah! Hey!" Shaking her shoulders doesn't raise her out of the stupor. Instead, she leans forward and pulls a long tearing bite from what I think is Levi's liver.

I think I'm going to be sick.

Well. She needs to be full. There's no time to dig a grave before she gets hungry again.

Gagging, I stumble away. Logic doesn't make this any easier.

Dry heaving in the driveway covers the hungry noises she makes.

Fuck this bile tastes awful.

When her growling and gnashing fades into crying, I know she's full.

"Caleb!" Her face turns to the sky. Fresh tears cut clean lines through the brown blood crusting across her mouth.

"Yea, baby. I'm here." When I lay a reassuring hand on her, she wraps her arms around my knee and cries against my thigh.

"Please, make sure you have a pistol. I don't ever want to find myself like this over you. Promise me, you'll leave a bullet in the chamber for me. Don't let me hurt you!" The words are staggered with gasping sobs.

"I promise. It won't get to that. Go get cleaned up and we'll go." Helping her to her feet, it takes every bit of willpower not to grimace in revulsion at the cloying smell of sour blood that clings to her.

Once she's clear of the garden fence on her way to the spigot, I take a hard look at Levi's remains.

She's ravaged his abdomen, pieces of entrails spill around his body like a fetid red aura.

I'm so screwed. I've barely scavenged enough to keep us fed for a day.

One last glance in her direction lets me know she isn't going to be back for a few minutes.

My pocket knife makes quick work of his arm. I manage to get the severed extremity shoved into my bag and tuck the stump under the blanket before she gets back.

That might buy me a little time.

What the hell is wrong with me? Cutting up my best friend to feed to his sister?

Happy wife, happy life.

Chapter 14

Jessica

Three damn days before my makeup reliably covers the bruises on my face. Every time I look at myself in the mirror, I wish I could go back to that horrific shack and slap Levi.

It took just as long to be able to shit without bleeding. But, with so little food in the house, that's becoming less of an issue.

My friends aren't answering any of my calls or texts. Levi ruined my life. They've completely cut me off.

Celeste is the one who really pisses me off. I brought her into my group. She *owes* me. Where does she get off ignoring *me*?

Bitch. I'll show her.

I'm single now. Nothing will stop me from showing up at her house and fucking her husband in front of her. He will throw her skanky ass out. Devon only married her because I told him no.

One more dab of mascara and I'm flawless. The extra puff in my lips is working to my benefit making them look like I just had filler put in.

Fabulous.

He won't be able to resist me. Devon may not be as rich, but once I take half of Levi's money in the divorce, Devon and I will have more than him.

It will serve him right to see us sitting closer to the front at the next country club meeting.

Everyone is ghosting me. I hate it.

Well, Brittney isn't. She's stuck on her family yacht off the coast of Cancun. Boo hoo. She married down to some construction worker and was on her honeymoon. I only talked to her long enough to get bored listening to her complain about not being allowed to leave.

At least she isn't trapped at a hovel with people that she hates. So, she has zero room to whine.

Gross. There's still blood and dirt on the front seat of the Land Rover. My Audi is on empty and the man who usually takes care of the cars isn't answering my calls either.

A clean towel works as a makeshift cover. I just can't let anyone see it.

Imagine if they did?

I would literally die from embarrassment.

God, these roads are terrible. So many cars are in the streets it makes it hard to navigate.

This is why I hate driving. But, my Uber app isn't working correctly.

It's like the whole world is against me.

Great. Some homeless person is stumbling in the middle of the street.

Wait. Is that a Louis Vuitton on her shoulder?

I bet she stole it. Ew. She got it all nasty, too.

Laying on my horn gets her to lose her balance, but she staggers back from nearly falling and stops. Her nappy head hanging low as she slowly turns to face me.

Her eyes are creepy. She looks like she's all drugged out like Veronica at her bridal shower. I told her not to go in the back with that male stripper. He was wearing a Gucci knockoff.

She should have listened. I can read a wannabe a mile away.

"Get out of my way!" My continuous honking isn't making me any progress.

I think it's making her get closer.

That girl needs a serious makeover. Her hair is all tangled, her face looks like she's been scratching at it, and I think she spilled red wine down her front.

Totally ruined that Ralph Lauren blouse she's wearing. Shame.

Really? Against my hood? Did she have to put her hands on my car?

"Bitch! I said move! Go do your cleanse elsewhere!"

No way.

Oh. That is too perfect.

It's Celeste.

"Well, well, well. Looks like you had a rough night. Too busy to call? Did Devon kick you out?" Both my hands land on the windowsill. I want her to see how marvelous my manicure is.

Her nails look hideous. They're broken and bleeding.

She groans and shuffles closer, her nasty fingers reaching out towards me.

So rude. She doesn't even reply.

"Celeste. You need your hair done. Your bangs are growing out, for real." With a tap of the accelerator, I pull away from her. If she won't even answer, I have no time for her.

Maybe that means Devon is home. I bet they had a fight if she's out here.

My timing is impeccable.

His house isn't nice as mine, there isn't a gate going into the culdesac. The neighbors are closer, but at this point I don't really care.

Someone needs to take care of me. If I have to look at an ugly house while the divorce is going through, so be it.

The lawn could use cutting. I wonder if Devon left? Levi would leave when we would fight.

He should have just left me like usual instead of doing what he did.

A shiver ricochets through me as I walk up the concrete path to the wide stone porch. I'm still sore from that night.

I hope he suffers.

The bell echoes through the large plate glass windows framing the door.

Where is he?

Rapping my knuckles against the heavy wood carries almost as far.

Whatever. He isn't home. I need to go to the country club. There's a chance that one of those old-money boomers will be lurking around. They're always looking for wife number eight or ten. But, they know how to take care of a girl like me.

"Jessica? Is that you?" Devon's voice cracks behind me.

Throwing on my brightest smile, I spin on my stiletto and toss my coifed hair over my shoulder. "Devon! How lovely to see you!"

He looks like shit. Are those sweatpants? And he's *dirty*. Dark bags under his eyes hide beneath shaggy, greasy hair.

"Jess. I'm glad to see you. Want to come in?" He lurches down the step. As he gets closer I can see how gaunt his cheeks are and his skin has a gray tone.

"Are you sick? I can come back later." My feet carry me backwards while he rushes towards me.

His hands wrap around my elbows in a fierce grip.

"No, I'm not sick. But, you're not going anywhere. I need you." Desperation burns in his gaze. We continue towards my Land Rover where he pulls the passenger side door open and pushes me in.

"Devon. What are you doing? I saw Celeste. She should be back soon." Well, I think she was going the other way. He doesn't need to know that.

"She got bit. I locked her out weeks ago. You're a fucking miracle." He crawls into the driver's seat and chirps the tires as he guns it into reverse.

"Where are we going?" This is *not* what I had in mind.

"I'm so damn hungry. You're going to help us get some food." He leans over the steering wheel as if his body weight will make us go faster. Clenching his jaws, his hips shift as we take a corner hard.

He's weaving in and out of the vehicles and debris littering the streets.

"Devon. Stop right now. Tell me what is going on." Batting at his arm doesn't seem to faze him.

"You'll see soon enough." His fingers tap on the steering wheel with nervous energy.

"Levi is going to come looking for me. I just came to see Celeste." He doesn't know Levi is still a hundred miles away.

"I thought you saw Celeste." He swerves around a garbage can toppled in our lane.

Shit. "Well, I was only parking for a minute. I was waiting on her to show up." I'm not at all interested in him now. He's acting like a crazy person and no longer a candidate for me.

"You've always been so full of it, Jess. A bratty bitch. I'm so glad you're here." His voice is hoarse and cracks every few words.

I never noticed, but his clothes are hanging off of his tall frame. He's so thin it's freaky.

No wonder Celeste left.

"Why are we going further into the city?" Malibu is on the coast, relatively quiet.

There's so much trash here.

"Don't worry. You'll be happy to know we're going to Beverly Hills." As if to accentuate his statement, he revs the engine making us jump ahead.

Well. That isn't so bad. I'll be amongst my own kind.

Signs start appearing on nearly every intersection. Big, bright letters spell out words that we're almost going to fast to read easily.

Safety.

Food.

Protection.

Haven.

I hope that's where we're going. Food and protection sounds fitting.

A heavy gate blocks the driveway he pulls us into.

I've never seen a man so big as the one who steps out of the guard shack. Two more men sit up on the high walls on either side.

Everyone has very large guns.

Devon rolls his window down.

He's bouncing. Weirdo.

"I brought one! Can I come in now? Please?" Devon gestures to the huge man lumbering closer.

"Let's see the goods." The brute's voice is so deep it vibrates through the floorboards.

My door flies open.

Yet another guy stands next to me and grabs my wrist, pulling me from my seat.

"What the hell? Do you know who I am?" This is not how I should be treated.

I barely see the lean figure touching me before I'm thrust back into the truck.

"She's not a mouth, but she's feisty." The handsy one calls over the hood before slamming my side shut.

"Can I get in?" Devon whines. He releases a noticeable sigh when the broad palm of the immense guard waves him through.

"Where are we?" I've never been here. The wide lawn is sprinkled with campers and tents. People mill around, some working in makeshift gardens.

It looks like almost all men. If having a woman is the price of entry, I bet they're all being well taken care of in the mansion.

Oh. Em. Gee.

I've never seen a building like that. As wide as I can see in both directions and at least four stories high, it's the most beautiful thing I think I've ever been this close to.

An older man in a fluorescent vest waves Devon over to where a line of vehicles are parked.

"Keys, please." He holds out his gnarled hand to Devon as we both get out.

"Can I have some food? I brought a girl." Devon sounds pathetic.

Rough hands tug my elbows and lead me up the main stairs to the elaborately carved main door. Two men are holding me firmly.

The entryway opens before we reach the top.

A tall, well muscled man with groomed blonde hair is standing just inside with a smirk on his face.

"Well, hello." His voice is gravelly as he brazenly looks me up and down. "Hungry?"

"No. You need to tell me what is going on." My foot makes a double click when I stomp my heel on the marble tiles.

Even my anger sounds elegant in here.

"Ah. Not a mouth. Tell me—" He slides forward with an air of arrogance that makes my belly long to be near the power he exudes. "—are you a whore?"

A quick glance around the room screams what my answer should be. Fine antiques, gold trim on every surface, and the scent of heavenly cooked meat wafting through the vaulted ceilings.

I put on my best pouty smile. "Of course not." I'm so glad I took off my wedding ring.

His suit moves over his body like it's painted on him. Expensive cologne spills over me when his fingers draw my chin up.

Left and right he turns my face, giving me a close view of him and the room beyond.

I recognize the look in his faded blue eyes. I see it in my own often. A different kind of hunger. The drive to dominate is a feral gleam reflecting back at me.

His smile is broad and gleaming, yet doesn't reach above his cheeks. "Welcome to my humble abode. I'm Peter."

Locked in a room with fifteen other women is not what I expected. Several of them are tied to beds and tables, their moans filling the room.

"No, you can't sleep here."

"Move, this is my spot."

"You have to earn a bed. Fuck off."

Pushed from empty space to empty space, I finally huddle on an unclaimed stretch of mattress sharing a bed with one of the tied women.

Apparently being so close riles her up, too. She starts thrashing and pulling at the ropes.

"Get away from her. She'll bite you!" One kinder voice erupts from the darkness.

I don't even care. It can't be worse than what I experience at the hands of Levi.

Besides, her rope is tight, and I'm exhausted. The best part about today was the full meal of delicious stew that Peter treated me with shortly after arriving.

He did tell me he thought I was so perfect, he wants to save me for later. After a fine dinner being waited on by his staff, it was an abrupt shock to be pushed into this room.

The promise is, if I'm not a whore, I get a better room.

Whatever that means. I'm not fucking anyone in here.

The growling and gnashing of my bedmate turns into white noise, the bouncing of the box springs almost like waves on a boat.

My eyes fly open to a room full of daylight, and pain radiating from my shoulder.

The bitch managed to roll over just enough to get her damn teeth on me.

I should have someone look at it. But, there's no way I'm going to let them think they were right.

As the day wanes, some of the women are escorted away. Not all of them return. The ones who do are hollow eyed and quiet after they shower, crawling directly into their beds.

No one asks them where they went.

By evening, my head is spinning and I'm fighting cold chills.

If the food wasn't so good, I probably wouldn't have been able to eat.

The second day passes in a haze. For the first time, I'm happy not being the center of attention. I don't want anyone to see how sick I am.

Pity is the last thing in the world I want.

They can all kiss my ass.

I start to feel better by dinner and wolf down the delicious bowl.

The moaning girl in my bed doesn't eat hers, so I take it. Besides, she doesn't shut up. This is payment for having to listen to her for two days.

Showering the morning of the third day makes me feel like I've shed my skin and regrown a new one.

I feel invigorated. The last of the puffiness in my face and soreness in my back is gone.

I'm even able to take a shit without it hurting.

Fuck Levi. He didn't break me.

Two bowls of breakfast barely fill me, but it's all I can manage to get my hands on.

"You." The dark complexion hides his leer as he points to me. "Boss is ready. Come with me."

Several of the girls have a look of fear flicker across their features as they drop their gaze away.

They're just jealous.

Sauntering past them feels like I'm a model on a runway. They all wish they could be me.

Wanted by Peter.

I won't be sleeping in this room again. I'll do whatever he wants me to.

Chapter 15

Sarah

Caleb guides me in and out of the fog of hunger. We've been walking for three days, but it feels like years.

I'm not sure how he fed me the first night, but I woke up that morning feeling refreshed and full. He shot a deer for me that afternoon with an impressive shot using the old twenty-two he found in the barn. It's what I've been gnawing on the last few meals.

Apparently, hungry me gives zero fucks if the meat is cooked or not.

"Maybe this one will still have gas?" he mutters as he pulls the door open on the fourth car this morning. Sliding the seat back, he folds his tall frame into the compact. It's almost cartoonish with how small it is.

At least we're finding vehicles. They're just all stalled out along the road because they're empty.

Two of them had bodies in them, long rotten. I guess when the hunger took them, they forgot how to get out. Like mindless mouths.

A shiver runs through me. I hate that I get that way. It's terrifying knowing I'm only one meal away from total loss of control.

And I'm running out of food. Whatever this is that's raging through me makes me much hungrier than normal.

"Shit." Defeat drips from his sigh as the engine fails to turn over.

We're still walking.

"I'm sorry, Caleb." The burn of tears sting my eyes before sliding down my cheeks. "If I hadn't been stupid enough to go in that bathroom without checking it, none of this would have happened." A sob chokes in my throat.

"Fuck, Sarah." His warm arms close over me and he kisses the top of my head. "This is *all* my fault. My lab created this monster. Do I regret making it? Absolutely." He leans back, his thumb raising my chin so I can look at him through my blurry eyes. "But, I'd have never found you. Do I wish things had gone differently? Goddamn right. We'll make the best of it though." His beard tickles when his lips land lightly on my nose.

It's the first time he's held me this closely in days. I've missed it. Burying my nose into the base of his throat, my fingers cling to his back while his palms rub warm paths up and down my shoulders.

"There's an older couple just another mile or so down the road. I think he had a fuel tank at his place. Maybe we'll find something around there that will work?" I don't want to rush away from this moment, but I can already feel the lightness in my stomach as it empties.

And, we're out of food.

"That's a great idea, baby. A mile isn't that far. Just keep talking to me, okay?" He grasps my hand in his and we start at a brisk walk.

The heat of the late summer sun is nearly at its peak when we reach the edge of a long gravel driveway leading to an old farmhouse. Overgrown fields are dotted with weed-bound equipment and trash.

"Do you think they still live here?" Caleb releases my fingers to pull the small rifle from his pack. "What are their names?"

My thoughts are foggy. I can see the images of their faces, but who they are floats just out of reach.

Shaking my head doesn't add any clarity. "I can't help on that one." Is this hunger or genuine forgetfulness? When was the last time I saw them? Five years? Ten?

Caleb turns and stares at me, his eyes narrowing. "Baby, I think you should wait here. I don't want to be explaining to them why you're trying to eat my arm."

Fuck. He's right.

A knot forms in my stomach before it growls.

I don't have long. Everything is getting fuzzy on the edges of my vision.

"Here, let me help you." His gentle words coax me through the haze and he takes my wrists.

But, as he steps away, it still feels like he's holding me.

Rope binds my arms together.

I'm just a little hungry. I'm not lost yet, am I?

"Come on, baby. Let's go this way." The heat of his palm warms beneath my elbow. Guiding me to a small shed filled with split logs, he drapes the end of the rope around a heavy beam and ties it off snugly. "I'll be back for you in a little while. Be good." Dropping a light brush of his lips to my forehead, he disappears past the edge of the wide doorway.

Slumping against the wall, I watch a parade of tiny ants work an ambling line disappear behind an old tire. If they were just a little closer, I could try one to see how they taste.

A hollow pain rides in my belly. He should have left me with a little food. Even a bite.

Wait. He did. Dried noodles? My hands move every time I try and pull off a bite. They aren't bad. Stiff. Dry. Stringy.

How long have I been here? I can hear the soft drift of voices followed by a bleating sound.

Like a goat. Goats have milk. That would taste good. My lips are dry from chewing on the...rope?

At least my hands are free.

So hungry.

Chapter 16

Caleb

I didn't have any choice but to leave her secure in that wood shed. The last thing I need is to have her trying to attack someone while I'm asking for their help.

If there's even anyone here.

Part of me hopes there is. The other half prays that there isn't. Grabbing just a few gallons of gas will get us to my lab.

That's all I need.

An acrid bite of woodsmoke hits me before I see the tendril waving up from the stove pipe.

Well, that answers that question.

"Hello the house!" I yell before stepping up onto the concrete porch. Today wouldn't be a good day to be mistaken for one of the infected.

My knuckles rap on the faded wooden door.

Patience has never been my strongest virtue, especially knowing that Sarah is waiting with an empty stomach.

"What do you want?" An older man's voice carries through the barrier.

"My name is Doctor Caleb Stevens. I'm friends with Sarah and Levi Hart that live a few miles down the road."

Pausing, I strain my ears to try and catch any indication he's going to shoot me.

No click of a hammer. Yet.

"Did you say 'doctor'?" There's a shakiness in his words as he asks.

Is this the advantage I need?

"That's correct. I am a doctor." The chance that I'm going to tell him it's in virology is zero.

Something heavy thuds against the wall before the knob twists.

A tired looking man in dirty clothes and unkempt hair leans on the handle, a weary look of relief on his face. "Our prayers have been answered. Please, Doctor, I need your help."

Glancing past him, I see a woman who seems to match him in age. She's huddling on a weathered couch, her hands knotted on her lap.

"I'll do my best. I'm looking for some fuel for one of the abandoned cars in the road." Stepping into the dim interior, the unmistakable smell of decomp singes my lungs.

Is there a dead body in here?

"Yea, I know. The stink is getting worse." He shakes his head and lowers his eyes to the floor. His bald top had dirt ringing the edges of his wispy white hair. "If you'd kindly follow me, I'll show you."

A double barreled shotgun leans against the wall. Dropping my bag next to it, I follow him as he shuffles ahead of me down a long narrow hall.

Groaning comes from the closed room ahead of us.

"I'm Mac, that was my wife out there. Her name is Helen. This—" He swings a battered door and a nauseating blanket of cloying rot hits me in a wave. "—is my daughter, Nelly."

It isn't that she's tied to the headboard that my sight catches first. Or, the short nightgown that has ridden up to reveal her naked lower half.

The extended abdomen of a late term pregnancy rivets my gaze.

She has to be full term.

"Holy shit." It slips out before I catch myself.

Nelly looks to be in her mid-twenties. And heavily infected. Her glassy eyes roll at the ceiling as a long and constant moan breaks through her dried, splitting lips.

A festering wound is covered with crusty bandages on the left side of her waist. That must have been where she was bitten.

Black threads weave beneath her skin as the gangrene radiates from the infected abscess.

Fat flies hang lazily in the air above her making slow circles.

"I've done everything I knew how to do. She showed up a month ago with a fresh bite." Mac runs a gnarled hand over his grizzled face. "I didn't know it'd be like this." He steps closer to the bed and gently touches the bound woman on her ankle.

Her scream sends a chill down my back as her head jerks forwards. Gnashing her teeth, her legs and arms writhe and tug on the restraints.

Mac steps away, but her lunges and snapping jaw take a few minutes to fade.

"Can she be helped?" His bushy salt and pepper brows hide the hope I know he has in his eyes.

When I shake my head, his mouth and shoulders drop at the same time.

"Do you think the baby is okay?" Burying his hands into his baggy jeans, he turns back to face his sick daughter.

"I don't know. There's a very strong chance it's infected, too. That's if it isn't already gone." I might as well tell him the truth. Without access to the internet, I have no way of checking if there's been any successful deliveries in these kinds of circumstances.

The long exhale he looses tinges the fetid air with the smell of sour tobacco.

"What do you want me to do, Mac?" I know what needs to be done. There's no coming back from this level of illness.

At least, not until I learn more about what is going on with Sarah and why she can regress from the hunger.

"I think, um. I don't know. Is she really gone too far to bring back?" Tears well and leave a clean path down his grimy face.

How much has he given up of himself for Nelly?

"There's no cure." I think I'm saying it for myself as much as him.

Reality tightens my throat. What if Sarah turns into...this? Would I be able to let her go?

Mac must feel the same. I see his Adam's apple bob as he swallows.

"Can we try and save the baby?" His lower lip trembles before he tightens his jaw.

Decision made.

"I'll help you with whatever you want to do. There's no way to anesthetize her. Or, induce labor. Without the proper sutures, there's a good chance she's going to bleed out. And, no guarantees that the baby will be healthy." Trying to rub my temples doesn't reduce the ache. "You know they both will likely die?"

"Tell me what you need, doc." Mac gestures at me to follow him. Picking up a notepad from the kitchen counter, he lays it flat, pen ready.

"Gloves, a sharp knife, needle and thread." Part of my training included some basics on medical procedures. But, I'm mostly flying blind.

"Give me two minutes." He folds the short list and puts it into his pocket. "Helen? Can you boil some water and gather some towels?"

She gives him a short nod as he paces across the room to the front door.

"Where are you heading?" A flare of panic courses through me. Sarah is still out there.

"The gloves are in the barn. They aren't those fancy hospital ones, but long ones I use for preg checking cows." One of his eyes widens larger than the other. "Will that work?"

Fuck. Nothing covering my hands means I might get sick. But, if he sees Sarah, she's as good as dead, too.

Maybe not. The shed is a good distance from the barn. There's a chance she'll stay quiet.

"Yea, those will work." Sweat prickles across my forehead.

I'm nearly on the verge of passing out from waiting when he comes rushing through the door, gloves in hand.

"Sorry, doc. They weren't where I thought they were. I found them in the shed."

What?

"The, um, one closest to the road?" Ice grips my heart and numbs my hands.

His chin dips as he drops everything on the counter. "I forgot I used them when I was greasing the tractor. Boy, that's a messy job!"

He didn't see her.

How in the hell do I get out of this quick?

Only one way, get the baby out.

"Okay, let's get this over with." The clear plastic gloves extend to my armpits, but I feel well protected.

Grabbing the knife, I head to the daughter's room.

She hasn't moved much.

"Mac, I'm going to need you to hold her hips as much as possible. She can't be twisting around so much." Why did I agree to this?

Mac moves pretty deftly for an older man. Tugging the sheet from the bottom of the bed, he wraps it around her legs like a burrito and then straddles her thighs, his firm hands pinning her pelvis to the mattress.

Nelly begins screaming again, the restraints on her arms taut with every movement.

"Okay, ready? I'm going to try and do this quickly." I don't know what the hell I'm doing.

Mac's face scrunches up. It's all the answer I need. The pain is a neon sign etched in his features.

When my palm touches her distended belly, I swear I feel something move inside. The blade pauses just against her skin when she rolls her shoulders and tries to buck Mac off.

"I'm good, doc. Let's just get it done." The old man's face is red with strain.

He won't last long.

One long slice across her lower abdomen leaves a trail of blackened blood spilling over the oozing gauze still attached to her side.

Is that how their fluids look all the time? Or is that the infection?

I wish I had paid closer attention in my medical training.

Peeling back the skin, another membrane is beneath it.

Two more long cuts and a gush of fluids spill all over us both.

Nelly shrieks and starts twisting. The knife falls from my hand, but closes around a tiny arm.

Tugging the purple infant free from the goo splashing around us, I almost drop it when it blinks at me.

"It's a boy," Mac exhales.

Sloughing some of the amniotic remains off of his face, the baby takes a deep breath for the first time. His toothless mouth falls open and a great cry fills the room.

My god. He's healthy.

A surge of hope envelops me. This could be mine and Sarah's. She can have a healthy child. He may even have immunities that could help prevent infection.

Adrenaline has my heartbeat thundering in my ears at all of the possibilities that have opened up with a slice of a knife.

"Doc? The umbilical cord. Cut it so we can get the heck out of here." Mac's voice has both excitement and resignation ringing through it.

"Yea, sorry." I can't reach the knife where it fell. Setting the crying baby on the edge of the mattress, I lean down to grab it.

Nelly slams herself back into the headboard with a crack. Her arm flies out and latches onto the face of her newborn son, ripping him from my grasp.

"No!" Mac dives forward across her belly.

But, his fingers slip on the wet skin.

Her teeth find the soft flesh of the screaming infant's belly as her hand squeezes tightly around his frail little neck.

The crying stops with a savage gurgle.

Mac's yell replaces his grandson's and he tears the knife from my hand before plunging it into the chest of his rabid daughter.

Over and over until she goes still.

Nausea overwhelms me and I stumble back, bile works its way free from my bowels.

It burns as I heave onto the stained carpet.

When the retching subsides, the only sound in the room is Mac's panting.

"I'm sorry." I don't know what else to say.

"It ain't your fault, doc. I thought she was bound. Didja see? He didn't look sick. I got to see my healthy grandbaby before I die." The soft words carry a suffocating weight.

Stripping the nasty gloves off, I can't leave the room fast enough.

This travesty still holds a seed of tomorrow's possibilities.

A pot of water simmers over the fireplace in the empty living room. Fresh towels sit on the end of the couch. It's too bad we won't need them.

So damn close though.

Mac closes the door and joins me in the living room. His arms and shirt are soaked in crusty blood.

"You should clean up so you don't get infected too." I make a broad gesture at his reddened hands.

How do I ask nicely for fuel? That shit show didn't go as planned, but I still need to take care of Sarah.

Maybe Mac has some extra food that I could give her to regain her hold on sanity while I'm trapped in the car with her.

"Helen?" His call echoes through the small house.

Washing his hands in a smaller bowl in the sink, he shrugs his shoulders. "She must be getting more logs for the fire. Probably good to clean up before she gets back." With a distant stare, he scrubs his palms together like he's on autopilot.

Impatience races my pulse, but I have to bide my time.

I just want to get the hell away from the carnage in the back room.

"Doc? After I break the news to Helen, would you help me with moving my daughter out? I know it's a big ask." A rag twists in his hands as he squints up at me.

A deep breath doesn't quell the anxiety churning my guts. "Yea, but then I really need to get going."

"I understand. You came at the right time." He tosses the damp cloth on the counter and glances around. "I'm gonna go see if I can find her."

Dread constricts my throat making my words come out with a croak. "Want me to come with?"

Mac's brows knit, but he gives me a silent nod.

My finger slips through the loop on my backpack as I pass. I doubt I'm ever going back into that house.

"Helen?" The last of the afternoon sun reveals the grime on Mac's pants. He looks like he's lived a hard few weeks. From the back, I can see where the waistband is folded over. How much weight has he lost to tighten them that much?

A soft sound grows steadily louder as we get closer to the shed I left Sarah tied in.

We're almost to the opening when it breaks through me what it is.

Crying.

There's two feet jutting out on the ground.

Every step reveals more.

A waist framed by bloody hands.

Sarah, kneeling over the body of Helen, her face and shirt covered in the glistening crimson proof of her last meal.

The old woman's throat and upper chest have been ravaged and torn apart.

"What the fuck?" Mac freezes in front of me. "Who are you?"

"I'm so sorry," Sarah sobs. Her teeth are still stained red, a glaring testament with every word.

"Are you...are you one of *them*?" Mac's hands shake at his sides.

Sarah's eyes well with fresh tears that spill down her cherry colored cheeks. Biting her lip, her chin drops to her chest.

What is he going to do? I don't want to kill him. If he makes a step towards her, I'll grab him.

Mac's shoulders slump and he turns on his heel. Brushing past me, his pace quickens as he gets nearer the house.

Shit.

"Sarah, we need to go." Rushing to her, I grab her elbow and pull her to her feet.

She stumbles with me, whimpering her apologies.

"Just run, we can talk later." We need to get the hell out of here before Mac comes back with his shotgun.

A muffled blast has me stopping.

Expecting to see Mac on the front step, it's a dark realization that his door is closed.

The single shot came from inside.

Fuck.

Chapter 17

Peter

I never thought I'd get bored getting everything I ever wanted.

Whores file in sniveling, crying, begging for mercy. It's tempting to start cutting out their tongues before they come in.

But, sometimes, one will surprise me.

This haughty bitch saunters in like she deserves to be worshiped. I let her stew for a couple of days with the other women to see if it knocked her down a notch.

It only enhances her arrogant stride when I call on her for dinner.

She acts like royalty. How can she look so put together when I know how sparse the quarters are? The golden locks of her hair are perfect, her skin is flawless, even without the makeup she arrived in.

But, those damn shoulders thrown back, her chin jutting, it makes my fingers itch to put her in her place.

"It's about time you brought me out of there. Those creatures are hideous." Her full lips flatten as one side of her mouth drops in a disdaining frown.

"Aren't you a saucy one? Might have to find out later if your ass has room with that stick up it." Sliding her chair out from the ebony table, I catch her slipping one eyebrow up as she sits.

"It isn't arrogance, Peter. It's the truth." She unfolds the heavy brocade napkin and spreads it primly across her lap.

The epitome of class. Tiny hairs on the back of my neck prickle as she looks down her nose at me with her big dark eyes.

Like she's fucking better than me. It's the same dismissive expression my father would wear when he locked me in the filthy cages of his fighting dogs.

I'm a mongrel. Worthless.

Rage festers into a knot in my guts while I yank my own ornate throne out.

This is a test to find someone to reign with me. She certainly has the attitude to make my cock throb against my zipper. I want to flail her, break her apart until she's begging me for mercy.

But, I want her to fight me every step.

It's more fun when they don't want it and I have to earn my victory.

"And what makes you so different from them?" My small silver bell next to my wine glass lets the server know I'm ready for the first course.

She's dessert.

"You don't know who I am? I'm Jessica Ha—" Her words are cut off by the waiter bursting in carrying a wide tray.

I'm quite fortunate that a renowned chef and maitre d from a five star restaurant requested sanctuary here in Haven.

Threatening their children ensures their abject devotion.

Her lips purse into a slight smile as the first course is set before her.

"Jessica who? Never heard of you." It makes my balls tingle seeing the flash of indignation before she composes herself.

Charlie and his entire chocolate factory could walk through the living room and I wouldn't recognize him. I've never been "in the know". Too busy fighting to survive.

"I'll have you know, there are millions of people out there who worship me." She raises a gilded fork and daintily cuts into the poached egg appetizer. "At least, before these *unfortunate* circumstances." Her tongue pokes out and welcomes the morsel between her full lips.

Fuck, her attitude makes me want to beat her. But, that mouth...

I want to cut it off and wear it like a cock ring.

As if in response, my pants tighten across the crotch. Yea, that's exactly what I'm gonna do if she's lying to me and turns out to be just another bratty whore.

"Are you even listening?" Her fat bottom lip protrudes in a pout.

Leaning back in my chair lightens some of the pressure from my throbbing groin. "You have a lot of balls. I'm surprised you haven't been slapped around."

Her eyes widen and she looks down to mess with her napkin.

Seems I found a chink in her armor.

When she smooths it back over her thigh, her features are neutral again. "I can assure you, that doesn't go over well."

Oh, there's a fire in her.

"What makes you think I can't do anything I want to you?" My hands fold around my plate. I'm not hungry for this shitty high class slop.

I want to skip to the after-dinner refreshments.

"You need me." Her tone is flat. She might as well be reading the states off of a map.

"Really? Enlighten me." Letting my fingers steeple against my chin, I love how she pushes her tits out with a deep breath.

"You need to have a front of welcoming to grow this little village. If your image is a single man who uses all the women who walk through, you'll never be more than a gang leader." She doesn't glance up as my servant pulls the empty dish from before her.

She doesn't even acknowledge him.

Elitism seeps out of her pores.

I hate that she's right. My rightful place in this world isn't as a common thug.

I'm a king. A damn Pharaoh rebuilding the pyramids in my own image.

"Why you? There's a hundred sluts here that would work." The braised salmon on my plate is getting cold, but I really don't care. She has my full attention.

Her eyes darken and her cheeks suck in as she purses those fucking lips. "I'm not one of them. I know "image" more than anyone else alive."

"Hmm." Shoving my chair back, I saunter to her end of the table and rest my hip against the corner. "You know what picture I have in my head right now?"

She doesn't flinch when my palm cups her jaw and my fingers dig in hard enough she opens that pretty, little mouth.

The bitch just raises one eyebrow like it's a Tuesday.

"Oh, no. You're going to bend the fuck over so I can see if you're worthy. Before one more word comes out of your throat, we need to find out if I'm keeping you." Gripping her cheeks firmly enough to squeeze her tongue, I rip her out of her seat and shove her face down across the large oak table.

"You're a fake, Peter," she garbles as I pin her neck to the polished wood. "An imposter." She pushes against the linen runner that lined the center, her hips rock lusciously against my swollen cock as she struggles.

"We're gonna find out if you are." Ripping up the edge of her skirt, the tearing sound her panties make sends a shockwave through my nuts. My frenzied pace pauses with one finger pushing into her slowly.

Well. Fuck me sideways.

She's actually a virgin. I've never found one this old before.

"You might just be worth keeping. You might not be a whore, but you're gonna be my slut." My fingers knot into her long blonde locks.

Her nails dig into my wrist, but it doesn't matter. Whatever she does, it'll heal back. She can't stop me from taking what's mine.

"You're an asshole!" One of the silver spoons bounces off her lips with each word before she tries to swing it at me. "Leave me alone!" The heel of one of her shoes catches my shin and digs tears through my slacks.

"That's going to cost you. I liked these fancy pants." Dropping my zipper, I free my raging cock. Already purple and swollen, her struggles push an ooze of pre-cum from the tip. "You're going to be my hostile bitch."

Her thighs shift and rub deliciously against me. It's only the scratching of her claws on my arm that keeps me from losing my load all over her round, pale ass.

It takes me two stabs to line up before I sink to my belly deep into her taut cunt. Her body tenses, clenching me impossibly hard as she looses a low sob.

Heaven.

"You're so fucking tight." Leaning over her, I can feel her hot panting reflecting off the table and it kisses the base of my throat. "I should cut a slit in you so all my friends can join."

She freezes and takes a shuddering breath. Splaying her palms on the elegant cloth, I can feel her entire body relax and go almost limp.

Did she pass out?

Jerking her head back, her wild eyes meet mine.

"No sleeping on the job, honey. I know you're fighting it. Go on. Tighten up that pussy for me. Or, do I need to cut you open and squeeze my own cock?" I can just reach the knife sitting next to my plate. Letting the tip trace the lobe of her ear elicits a quiver through her body as a fat tear drops down the edge of her flaring nostril.

There it is. Renewed pressure draws my pulsing length deeper within her.

"That's my good girl. I'm going to make you my second in command." That did it. Her cries shift to breathy gasps as I drive into her. "I'm going to put you in charge of the entire community."

Her cheeks darken in a flush as my balls slap wetly against her dripping cunt.

She is like me, getting off on the power.

"You're gonna be my cum sponge." God, I'm so close. A tingle builds in my belly as my abs begin to spasm. "But, you're also gonna be my queen."

Her scream does me in as her body seizes me in a convulsing orgasm.

Jesus. Fuck. I didn't know women could feel like this. Fire explodes from my cock as I spurt into her. My climax tears through my body in shivers before my legs give and I collapse over her.

With my heart still pounding heavily in my ears, I pull myself off of her and slide out. Cum dribbles down her thigh onto her tattered underwear still laying on the floor between her feet.

Still prostrate across the table, her breathing evens. "I'm not going back with those filthy vermin. Where is my new room?"

My dick twitches at her unbroken defiance. I'll enjoy trying harder.

"Upstairs on the right. It's even done up in purple. Fitting for royalty." I give her my most charming smile as she turns towards me.

I don't see the flash of the knife until her arm almost completes its arc. The blade slices down across my stomach and embeds itself into the hilt of my exposed semi-hard dick.

With one hard yank, she cuts it in two.

Agony knocks me to the floor as blood floods between my fingers.

She stands over me writhing beneath her.

"There's a new boss, bitch." Turning on her heel, she walks beyond the edges of my fading vision.

Chapter 18

Sarah

I fucked everything up.

And, Caleb is a saint for dealing with me.

We loaded up the sedan the old couple had parked in their garage. Ironically, it had a full tank of gas. There was plenty of food in the house, so at least we don't have to worry about me lapsing again.

Hopefully.

"Fuck." Caleb's fist bounces off the worn leather steering wheel as the car sputters and dies.

"How much farther?" It seems like we've been driving for hours. We've got to be close.

His hands clasp together and he drops his forehead to rest on them. "Just twenty more miles." With bloodshot eyes he glances up at me.

I tried to give him a break, but he didn't want to switch. He hasn't slept in days.

Tucking my fingers between the heat of his thighs, I give his leg a little squeeze. "Maybe we should just stay here tonight. It's late, but there's lots of food."

So, at least one night of me not trying to eat him. The thought makes my stomach roll, though not with hunger.

Everything this man has done, it's been to help me.

I feel inadequate.

We're in the middle of nowhere, the barren Nevada landscape stretches in every direction. Flat. Unforgiving. Empty.

"I'll get the tent. It was a good idea putting it in." A little pang of guilt darts into me as I climb out of the beat up car. I was telling him we wouldn't need that dirty thing when he found it in the barn.

Good thing he didn't listen to me.

"I wish we didn't need it. Dammit." He slams the door closed hard enough the chassis rocks on squeaky suspension. Scratching his long fingers through his dark wild hair, he lets out a lengthy sigh before reaching into the trunk and grabbing a bag. "Yea, sleep will help."

He follows me to a relatively bare spot in a field of sage brush and scrub to unceremoniously drop his cargo.

As we're both walking towards the dead sedan, he tugs at my elbow, turning me to face him.

"Baby, I'm sorry. I was hoping we'd make it today." The muscle of his jaw starbursts up to his temple as he clenches it. "I just really wanted to make it to the lab." His arms wrap around my shoulders and he snugs me into his hard chest.

Tears well against my nose and drip down my cheek. It feels so good to be in his embrace.

Warm. Comforting. Like it's us against the world.

I haven't felt this for a few days.

"Thank you." I hope he knows it's for the hug. For a little dose of love when I've been doubting us and myself ever since the fire. For sticking with me even when I ruin everything.

I want to melt into him and offer up what little good is left in me.

It's hard to let go when he pulls away, taking long strides back to the dilapidated vehicle.

Within the next trip, we get everything we have for our meager camp.

The little propane stove kicks off almost enough warmth to cut the chill of the high desert night. It also makes the ridiculous amount of corned beef taste somewhat palatable as it boils in a two gallon pot over the blue flames.

Gagging down the mushy meat, it does little to fill the hole in my chest that only grows as I mull over the events of the last few days.

I'm a monster.

The shiver that runs through me taps my spoon against the metal rim of the pot making Caleb look at me sideways.

"Come here, baby. You look cold." He peels the blanket back that he had wrapped around his shoulders to beckon me to join him.

It wasn't the temperature that caused the goosebumps to erupt over my arms, but I won't turn down his invitation.

Nestling between his strong thighs, I lean into the heat of his body.

He just feels so damned good.

"You know—" His beard tickles against my ear as his warm breath washes over me. "—it was the perfect set-up at the cabin." His chin props on the back of my head as he turns his face to the sky. "I was thinking about how maybe we could find a goat and some chickens. Do you think maybe after we're done at the lab, you'd like to live on a farm?" He wraps his arms around my waist, snugging the blanket across my legs.

"I'd love to live on a farm. Maybe some pigs, too? I've always wanted a pig. Their noses look easy to boop." One of my students would draw their snouts as a doodle on all of her homework pages. She said it was her favorite animal.

"Mmm, bacon." His throat rumbles and vibrates my skull.

Heat simmers in my belly. I'm not sure if it's his growl or the thought of fresh salted pork that causes it.

"Do you think we'll ever have a normal life again?" I can't help but voice the fear that lingers under my every thought. The idea of living like this forever is, well, daunting. Terrifying.

Abhorrent.

I don't want it.

The silence stretches through several of his long breaths.

"We will. We'll have a houseful of kids, with a puppy and an angry rooster that likes to chase us around when we collect eggs." His laugh ruffles my hair in short, warm waves.

"That's a nice dream." I drown my sorrow in the food in front of me. He's wrong, I'm sure of it. But, I can't bring myself to sour the hope.

The lab will do that soon enough.

When the little flame of the stove begins to sputter, he helps me to my feet so he can spread out our blankets.

I'm not sure how I feel about him falling to sleep after only a kiss to my forehead. His talk of children doesn't match the platonic peck he gave me.

It makes it hard to rest. Every horrible scenario runs through my head.

He must not love me. As soon as we get to the lab, he's going to strap me to a table to do experiments. Or, he'll leave me there with a pack of cold scientists who will only use me for their tests.

Maybe he won't? His hand wrapped over my waist doesn't give me the impression he's running away quite yet.

As the morning sun starts peeking through the thin canvas of the tent wall, he snorts mid-snore and turns onto his back, binding the blanket around his wrist.

It exposes his abdomen with its dark line of hair leading from his belly button to the hem of his boxers.

I can just see the tip of his flaccid dick poking out of the gap in the fabric.

Perhaps a happy wake up will change his mind? The need for his desire burns within me.

Fuck it.

Rolling over, I stealthily fold back his open fly and seal my lips around the soft head. Tasting him, I let my tongue swirl around the ridge and tickle his tender shaft.

I kinda like it when he isn't hard and huge, gagging me as he thrusts. This is the first time I can take him all in.

My mouthful grows. A groan escapes his lips as his hips move.

As his erection firms, it's so difficult not to choke. But, I want to hold him as deep as I can.

His fingers knot in my hair. "Mmm, Sarah."

A gasp escapes him as he clenches his fist, jerking himself free of my suctioning cheeks. "Sarah! What the fuck? Are you awake or trying to chew my dick off?"

He half holds me up by my burning scalp.

Goddamn it hurts. "Caleb. I'm sorry. It's me." How could I be so stupid?

His head drops against the ground with an echoing thump. The tension of his hold releases so I can shift away.

My cheeks are so hot they burn. The cool fabric of my pillow helps slightly as I bury my face.

If only I could suffocate so I didn't have to deal with this.

"Jesus. You have simultaneously fulfilled a dream and a nightmare." His bare stomach quivers with his low laugh.

His touch almost startles me as his palm drifts down my body to settle at my hips. "I'm sorry, baby. I didn't mean to pull your hair."

Peeking one eye over my elbow, I can see the concern knitting his eyebrows.

"I wasn't thinking. I just—" My teeth dig at my lower lip as I try to muster the words. "—I just want you to fuck me while I still know who I am."

There, I said it. Now, I can hide and attempt to smother myself again.

I can hear the blanket flip away before his weight settles over me, scalding me with his heat.

"I wasn't sure if you wanted to." The bristles of his dark beard tickle against my neck as his thigh wedges between my knees, spreading my legs to accommodate his lean body.

His need presses between my ass cheeks. "I have a hunger, too." His husky voice vibrates through my skin.

It feels as if my heart changes its rhythm to answer. "You do?"

"Mmhm. One which only you can sate." Sinking his teeth into my sensitive lobe, he shifts to pull my panties from my waist.

The tip of his rigid cock puts pressure against the edge of my slick pussy, but he stops.

Teasing me.

Fire races through my veins as his hot fingers push beneath my waist. When his seeking touch connects with my throbbing clit, the shock makes my hips buck involuntarily.

"Please..." The word squeaks out as he strokes an inferno within me. I want him to fill the empty ache that has left me hollow inside. To overflow the void that has formed over the last few days where my humanity used to be.

"You are my craving, Sarah." His engorged length rubs harder, the thick head broaching my tight entrance as his hand pushes my pelvis up to meet him.

It's like the first time. He stretches me with each thrust as he slowly drives himself into me. I can feel the ridge of his mushroomed head dragging along my quivering walls as he pistons.

Tightness builds deep in my belly, layered and growing with each rhythmic caress.

"Always?" I long for him to keep me, despite my new appetite.

"I will devour you forever, baby. My never ending smorgasbord." His body tenses over me and his breathing shortens to pants. "Come for me, Sarah. Let me consume you."

The coil inside me explodes in a pulsing wave. Screaming into the pillow doesn't dampen the sounds of his grunt as he follows me in ecstasy.

His hips spasm before he rolls off of me, his arm flinging across his eyes. "My god, I've missed that." A pant punctuates each word as his sweaty palm flattens over my naked ass cheek.

My eyes droop as I fall into my pillow. It feels good to have my heart billowing and happy once again. I was so worried that my recent meals might have turned him off.

He's even still moaning.

I know it was amazing, but why is he still making that noise?

Blinking against the brighter light, he's moved his hand down to press a finger to his own lips, motioning me into silence.

A low groan drifts through the thin walls of our shelter. Shit.

As quietly as I can, I grab up my pants and slip my hoodie over my head. Caleb dresses quickly next to me, grabs the rifle, and unzips the door.

"Hurry, Sarah. There's too many." His hushed words are laced with panic as he shoves his bare feet into his boots.

I have to take some food. I like being *me*.

"Now!" He stumbles backwards, the barrel pointed beyond the tent.

Shuffling sounds grow louder.

Ducking under the low door with four cans of corned beef, it is impossible to miss the small crowd of infected stumbling towards us. There's at least twenty of them, in torn and ragged clothes, most missing their shoes.

They're all the same size, kids. Maybe elementary school?

A pang hits me as I instinctively look for any familiarity in them.

I miss my own class.

"Let's go!" Caleb grabs my elbow and we start jogging away.

Leaving all of our gear.

"How are there so many?" I can't even fathom all of those poor parents out there.

"There was a sign for a school a mile or so back." He glances over his shoulder as he talks.

They aren't gaining.

"And they're still running in a pack? It's been months." My legs are still wobbly from my orgasm, but panic is pushing me.

"Bet they finally ran out of bodies. School probably had a stocked cafeteria." His boots beat against the hard pavement setting an easy pace.

The hungry children fall farther behind.

"Damn. I was hoping most had starved out by now." My eyes drop to the ground as my own words haunt me.

I'm one of *those* things.

Chapter 19

Jessica

I can't believe how soft these sheets are. It's almost like I've been sleeping in a shack for the last few months and I've finally returned home.

Peter is obviously not born into this lifestyle. Yea, he's hot in a feral kinda way. But, I bet he was a dog off the streets and took advantage of this place.

What I don't understand is why it hurt when he fucked me. Like it was my first time all over again.

It's probably because he's an animal. He's so trashy, now that I think about it.

I wish I had been able to meet the real owners of this divine house. They would have welcomed me with open arms.

If I still had my phone, I'd google them. My fingers twitch with emptiness. It's almost like I'm naked without it.

But, I'm too tired to care. There's even a full wardrobe of women's clothes, pressed and clean.

O.M.G. There's Stefano Ricci. The most fabulous silk I've ever felt.

Heaven.

I could totally die right now in bliss. Levi never bought me anything this amazing.

Screw him. I hope he's happy with the ashes of his peasant hovel.

I'm a queen.

The harsh glare of the hall lights sear across the comforter as the heavy door of my room is flung open hard enough to bounce off of the wall.

"You fucking bitch."

Shit. It's Peter.

His blonde hair is disheveled and his suit is covered in blood.

"You should have just let me fuck you," he growls as he paces across the room. The glint of reflection off of the knife in his hand has me scurrying beneath the covers.

I can't get out of the bed away from him fast enough. His rough grip tangles in my hair and jerks me backwards across the mattress before letting me bounce on the hard floor.

But, he doesn't stop. Dragging me down the hall, every stair rakes my spine and bruises my hips.

"Let me go!" Clawing at his hand does nothing to slow each agonizing jolt of the marble edges.

"I didn't want to get blood all over my pretty guest bedroom. So, now you've earned a special surprise." He lets out a chilling laugh.

Flailing, I snag one of the banister posts with my fingertips.

My scalp screams and feels like it's ripping from my skull as he continues his downward steps.

Two of my nails break, tearing into the quick as they fall free of my handhold.

It's several more jarring drops until we hit the smooth floor of the foyer.

The light from the house follows our path before abandoning me when he crosses over the course gravel.

Screaming doesn't lessen the fiery burn of the rocks scratching across my ass and legs. "Help me! Someone? Please?" There has to be one person in the shanty camp that will save me?

"Yell all you want, whore. They know the deal when they show up. I do whatever I want." He stops next to one of the campers in the yard, raising the large knife and pounding on the side with the butt of it.

"Jeremy! Open your fucking door, you worthless piece of shit!" Peter's deep voice echoes across the encampment.

A dull yellow washes over me and I can hear the footsteps from beneath the frame.

Maybe he'll help me.

"Peter. What can I do for you?" It's the waiter's voice from dinner.

Why did he drag me to a servant?

That is irritating. I'm better than that.

Twisting my body only makes Peter's knuckles tighten, yanking more hairs loose from my head.

"You rotten fuck. You left me laying on the floor bleeding out after this bitch sliced me. So, you're giving me your daughter, or your wife. I'll be nice enough to let you choose." He taps the frame with the tip of his blade like the metronome I used for piano lessons when I was a kid.

God, I hated those.

"Sir, I apologize. But, I knew you'd be fine. Your healing is unprecedented." There's a quiver behind his words.

What is he talking about?

"Doesn't matter. You left me. Choose. Or, I will." Peter steps into the opening, his foot landing on one of the small metal stairs.

He doesn't seem to care that he's bouncing my head off of the aluminum siding.

A raspy cry comes from deeper in the camper before another set of footsteps joins our little party.

"I'll do it." The voice is almost robotic.

Peter lifts me so my knees hover above the dirt before lowering his twisted face level with mine.

"If you try to get up, I'm cutting those tight hamstrings so you'll never walk again." His blue eyes are tinted with red as he stares at me.

"Fine." I can bide my time.

The woman that steps from the trailer is so thin she almost disappears in the dim light. Her gaunt legs wobble as her husband holds her hand so she can descend.

Her head scarf is hideous.

What the hell is wrong with her neck? She has a gaping hole at the base of her throat that puckers and widens with her breathing.

Eww.

"Show this cunt how to give a blowjob." Peter shoves the woman to the ground next to me making something small and metallic clatter away into the darkness.

"Please, sir—" The waiter tries to follow his wife before Peter waves him back with the pointed blade. "—she's been especially sick. I think her cancer came back."

"Well, you shoulda thought about that before you left me to bleed out." He unzips his blood caked pants.

I must have hit my head harder than I thought when he bounced me down the stairs.

"That's right. Look at what your crazy ass did." He grabs my hair and pulls my face close to his crotch. "Sliced my dick right in half. Well, joke's on you. It healed into *two* so I can fuck you twice as hard." His rough hand cups my jaw and his fingers dig into my cheeks, forcing my mouth open.

Both giant cocks bob engorged in front of me.

What the fuck?

"You and Susan here are gonna have a little contest to see who can outlast." He puts the tip of his cold knife flat on my protruding tongue. "And if I feel your teeth, I'm running this through the top of your head."

Releasing my tangled locks, his palm flattens over the woman's head, pushing the gaudy cover off of her bald scalp.

She has a flash of terror cross her withered features before she opens her mouth obediently, letting him thrust deep into her throat.

Tears push from her eyes, but she doesn't move.

Mucus-laden gurgling breaths are all I can hear over the soft squish of his dick being forced into her.

"Take it all. Show her your little trick." Peter grabs her by the back of the neck and pistons his hips forward. One of his erections press against her leaking eye as the other tip appears through the crusted orifice in her throat.

"Abracadabra. Tickle my cock, bitch."

Shit. He's talking to me.

With a shaking hand, I reach out and touch his slimy head through the ragged hole.

Brown and green phlegm oozes from her unnatural cavity as she tries to cough around the intrusion.

"No. With your tongue. Taste me while I'm in her throat." He pulls back just enough that he unblocks her opening allowing a rush of air to bubble in.

"That's fucking disgusting. Can't I just suck on the other one?" I'll do anything he wants at that point.

She's *gross*. Kinda stinks like she's rotting from the inside out, too.

"You will. But first I want to gag two whores with one cock." His free member wags as he laughs. "Hey, Jeremy!

Maybe you should send out your daughter so I can choke three at once!"

"She's only twelve, sir." There's a growl in Jeremy's tone. He shifts to fill the door, blocking more of the weak illumination.

"Yea, whatever. I'll save her for next time." He waves his hand nonchalantly before it lands on my shoulder.

Shoving my face at the foul void above her collarbones, I fight the nausea rolling in my stomach.

Oh, God, it smells worse as I get closer.

Her body convulses as he shoves himself deep enough to impale her.

"Now," he grunts.

I've never been more grateful that the phones stopped working and no one will see this.

Sticking my tongue out, I seal my lips around her gaping hole tightly before closing my eyes.

Everything is slick with mucus. I can't distinguish where he ends and she begins.

Bile rises in my throat as I lick his mushroomed head. Salty pre-cum mixes with the noxious fluids that coat my mouth.

"More." His hips move, driving his swollen cock in and out of her throat.

Susan's thin fingers push against my thigh as her shoulders jerk.

When I back off, a whisper of her breath moves past my cheek.

Peter's growl makes us both tense up. "I didn't say you could stop."

The butt of the knife digs into the back of my skull as he forces my mouth back over her neck.

If he would just finish, maybe he'd leave us alone.

That invigorates me. My tactic changes from hesitation to a frenzied attack, swirling and sucking as best as I can.

Susan's grip loosens as Peter's thrusts get harder.

"Fuck, I'm gonna shoot down both of your throats. Suck harder." The press of the weapon disappears as he strokes his other cock.

He swells and spasms as a hot burst spurts out of him. Mixing with her fetid lung juice, I can't hold back and vomit without moving the seal of my mouth from her skin.

"Oh. Goddamn. That was so rank." He withdraws himself and grabs a handful of my hair, wrapping it around his dick and covering me in phlegm and chunks of salmon.

He lets me sit back on my heels, but I fall onto all fours as the rest of my stomach contents decide to appear.

The woman collapses, unmoving.

A nasty mix of fluids seep from the hole above her still chest.

Peter adds a stream of urine, dousing her unblinking eye and it floods the growing puddle of sewage on the ground. "Well, got the best head of my life, guess I don't need her anymore."

We must be done. He's zipping himself up.

I want off of this hell ride.

Why can't I go back to the parties, the bars, the dance clubs with my friends?

This new world sucks.

Well fuck my life. His fingers knot against my numb scalp and he drags me away from the camper.

Jeremy plummets down the steps, collapsing next to his dead wife.

"Next time, you'll know where your priorities sit," Peter calls back over his shoulder. "Don't forget you have a daughter."

"What are you going to do to me? I've learned my lesson." Will tears work on him? I'm willing to try anything at this point.

Sobbing makes him stop.

"Your crying is fake, just like you. Prissy bitch. Time to spread you wide for the whole world to see you for the cunt you are." He picks me up roughly and pushes me backwards.

Landing with a hollow metallic thud, my head bounces off of a rod.

The whole world shifts as I rotate from the force.

What is this thing?

"Looks like I need this. Too bad, the color looked good on you." He fists my beautiful silk shirt, popping all of the buttons, and tears it from me.

Biting the hem, he rips it into strips.

"Lay down."

Cold steel burns against my back as I try to cover myself with my hands.

How is it turning?

One of my ankles gets jerked to the side and tied to a pole.

Then he stretches my legs uncomfortably wide to tether the other.

He pushes on one of the uprights and I turn a full revolution so my head is looking up at his thighs.

Shit. It's one of those kid's merry-go-rounds.

With bruising force, he pries my arm away from my breast and lashes it to another post.

It isn't long before I'm strapped down, spread eagle to the chill of the night.

"I kinda want to fuck you like this. Ever had two peckers at once? I bet with that stick up your tight ass, it'd only be a needle-dick mosquito fucker that would fit." He strokes his crotch slowly before letting me spin a few times until I slow to a stop with my feet near him.

"Please, let me go. I won't try anything again." I can just make him out against the darkness.

"How about, no."

The tip of the knife plunges between my legs and spears into my asshole to the hilt.

Pain.

I've never experienced agony like this.

Screaming doesn't help as he saws upwards until he hits the bone.

Blood pours in a burning lake around my hips and spread thighs.

"See. I might be a hick at heart—" He pulls the blade out and holds it point down over the front of my pelvis. "—but I know how to gut a deer." With his free hand, he hits the hilt, driving the tip in with a cracking misery that makes spots appear in my vision.

My throat burns as my voice rips out of my body.

"I figure it's only fair." He wiggles it until I can feel my hips shift apart. "You cut my shit in half, now I returned the favor."

I can't hear anything else. My ears are deaf from my own wails.

It's so loud, it blinds me.

At least the warmth of my own blood offers some comfort.

Like a blanket, muffling the world.

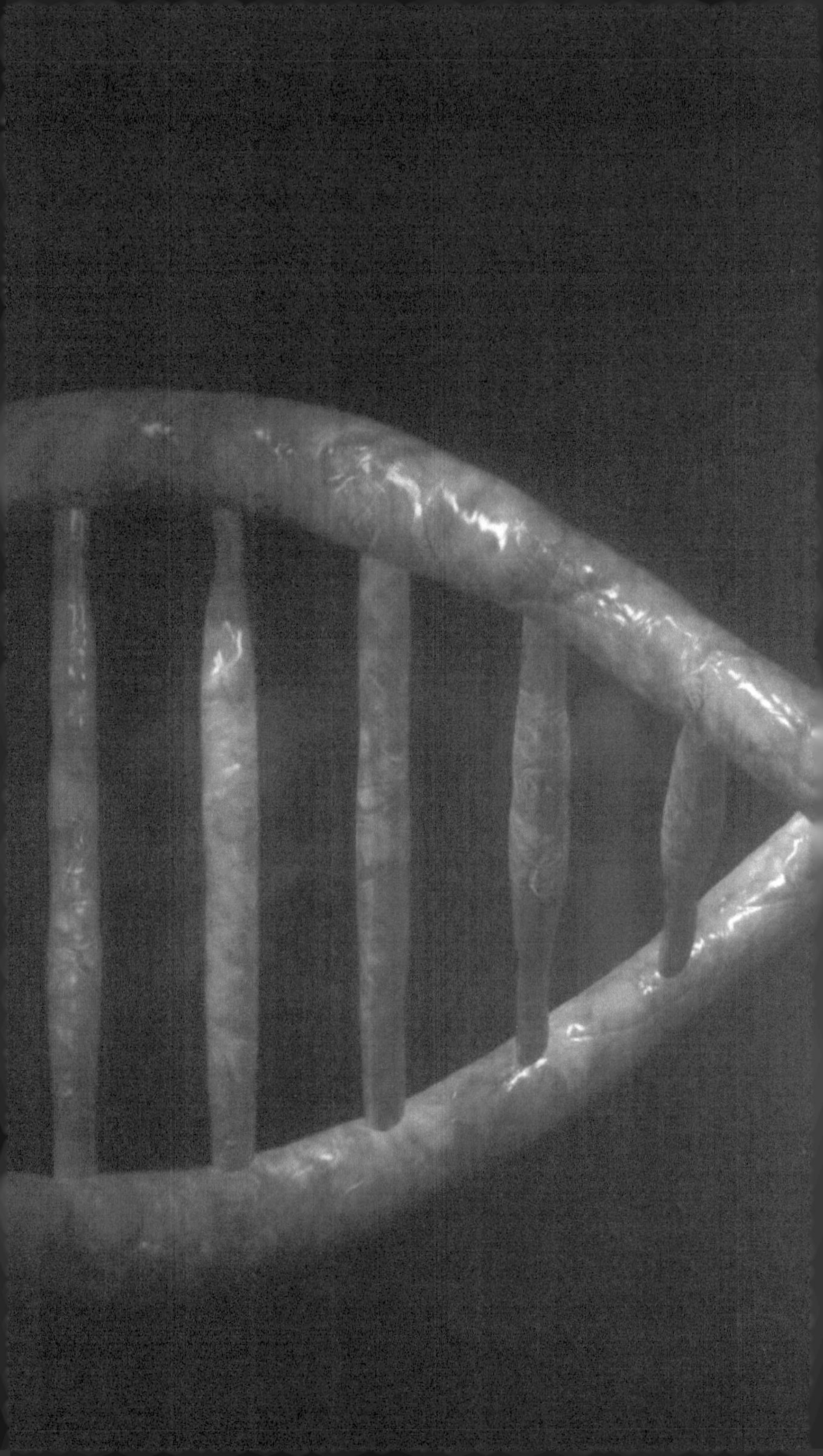

Chapter 20

Caleb

"Caleb?" Her voice sounds tired.

We've been pushing hard all day. First was to get away from the ravenous kids. Now, it's a race to see if we can get to the lab before her food runs out.

The research facility was purposefully built in a remote location due to the dangerous nature of our studies.

But, the barren surrounding makes for very meager pickings for food.

"Yea, baby?" My footsteps slow so she can catch up. She's been falling farther behind. I'm worried that I know why.

"I-I'm out of corned beef." The clink of the empty can bouncing off of the hard asphalt adds emphasis to the impact of her words.

"It's okay. We're almost there. Only another five or six miles I think." Tugging her palm into mine, I fall into the rhythm of her steps and wrap my arm around her shoulders. "You're such a good girl. I know this has been hard. You can do this."

After dropping a soft kiss on her temple, we walk in silence for a long time. The hillside that the lab is built against looms in the distance, but never seems to get any closer.

As the sun begins to kiss the horizon, she falls to a stop.

"What's the matter? We're almost there." I try to pull her forward, but she doesn't follow.

"I'm hungry. Leave me here before I can't control it." Her chin falls to her chest. Large tears plop onto the dry ground at her feet.

"Don't be ridiculous. You might get a little bitey, but I'm still going to keep you." Tugging her against my sweaty chest, I tilt her head to taste her. She still has a flavor of canned meat on her tongue. "Besides, I can put babies in you even when you turn completely. I've seen it."

Her emerald eyes scrunch at the corners and those full lips purse, begging me to lean over to nibble on them. "You'd fuck me when I didn't know I was me?"

I give her my best grin. "Of course. You'd be like a walking sex doll. Blow jobs would be off the table though." My palm cuts through the air, parallel to the ground in a sweeping gesture.

But, a big smile breaks over her troubled features. "Deal. Use me baby. At least I know I'll serve a purpose."

Cupping her elbow with light pressure, it's enough to get her moving with me.

"Heck yea. My own personal fuck toy. Always wanted to buy one of those pocket fleshlights, but never got around to it." I give her ass a light swat. "The real thing is so much better."

"What happens—" She pauses, watching the ground pass beneath our steps. "—if I accidentally bite you?"

"You already did." I didn't want to tell her. But, maybe it will offer her some peace of mind. "That first night, after Levi..."

She freezes, turning to me. Her thin fingers fly to her paling cheek. "No!"

"It's already healing, see?" Lifting my shirt, I thread my arm out of the hole so she can see the small scabs left by her teeth just inside my armpit. "I didn't get sick."

"Oh, Caleb! Why did you hide it?" Her touch is cool as it traces the marks.

My shoulders rise and fall in a shrug. "We already had enough going on. I didn't think it would help to worry you." I slip my sweatshirt back down. "I figured if I turned, we'd just wander together."

A tendril of her dark hair waves against her cheek, so I reach out and tuck it behind her ear. "I told you, you're mine. Can we get to the lab now?"

With a quivering chin, she gives me a short nod before taking my hand.

The main building is just coming into view when her dragging steps shift and her nails dig into my arm.

"There's my little monster." My hand presses against her chest.

With glazed eyes and drooling mouth, her teeth click with each snap as she tries to bite my arm.

Holding her at bay, I slip my belt from the loops and manage to catch both of her wrists.

This actually makes it easier. Keeping hold of the free end, I'm able to almost jog ahead while she tries to chase me down.

Apparently food is a good motivation.

The fact that there are several vehicles in the parking lot means someone is likely here.

Flipping her around, I pin her against my body as I reach the entrance and press the buzzer.

It takes forever, but a voice finally comes over the speaker.

"I'm sorry, this is not a shelter. The nearest one is in Reno." A woman's voice with a soft accent comes through the static.

"Carmen? It's Caleb." Fuck it's nice to hear her voice. She might be a hard ass boss, but she's brilliant.

The lock frees and I'm able to push through into the illuminated hallway of the concrete building.

Sarah's low groan echoes through the foyer as she struggles against me. With her head swinging back and forth, she tries to bite my arms.

"No, don't bite, baby. I'm taking care of you." With a firm hold of my belt, I head in the direction of the staff cafeteria.

I'll break one of the damn vending machines if I have to.

"Caleb!" Carmen approaches almost soundlessly. I didn't hear her without her heels on. "What the hell? You brought one in?" Her hands fly up and she stumbles backwards as Sarah's attention turns to her.

"Yea, but she's special. Is there any open food? I need to get her eating something, then we'll talk." My pace doesn't slow as I drag Sarah away from Carmen.

"There better be a good reason for this, Caleb. Do you know how dangerous she is?" Carmen hustles ahead of me, her white lab coat billows around her thin frame as she moves.

"I do, Carmen. I've been out there for the last few weeks living in the hell we created." Holding Sarah in place, I watch as Carmen digs through one of the commercial refrigerators lining the huge kitchen.

With the number of vehicles, I expected more people to be milling around.

"Where is everyone?"

Her dark hair cascades over her shoulder as she turns to face me. "Some were helicoptered to Vegas. They think they had a breakthrough."

"There's a cure?" My heart races in my chest.

Maybe there really is hope.

"Not yet. But, we have been able to muster some reversal of symptom severity in select cases. Someone in Vegas stumbled on an aberration in the viral mutation. They're running tests on the subject as we speak." She turns and pushes the heavy steel door shut with her foot while balancing a tray of sliced deli meat and cheeses.

It looks delicious, but I can wait.

Sarah doesn't. As soon as the heaping pile is pushed close enough on the counter, she bends at the waist and drops her mouth to begin gulping in huge portions.

Carmen crosses her arms and tilts her head as her mahogany eyes narrow at Sarah. "I don't see what the point of this is. She's too far gone. The only success we've had were ones very early in progression. I'm sorry Caleb, this one can't be helped."

"Just relax, Carmen. She's why I'm here." I steal a chunk of cheese from the corner of the platter since my own stomach is growling.

Well, Sarah didn't try to bite my hand. That's progress.

Her frantic gulping slows and she starts picking up individual slices of ham and rolling them up before chewing on them.

"Sarah? Can I remove the belt now?" When I put a light touch on her lower back, she straightens and nods with puffed cheeks.

"You look like a hamster, baby." The weight on my shoulders lifts as my girl looks over her shoulder at me with a guilty expression.

"Sorry." She covers her bulging mouth with her fingers and swallows before holding her wrists out.

"Holy fuck." Carmen's arms have dropped to her sides as she stares open-mouthed.

I don't think I've ever seen her eyes that wide.

"I gotta get Steve. We need blood samples. Yesterday." She takes off in a jog across the cavernous dining hall before disappearing beyond the double doors.

"What did I miss?" Sarah picks up a small handful of snacks and sits down in the closest chair before pulling her knee up to her chest.

My palms frame her face and I put a soft kiss on her forehead. "I'm always happy when you come back to me. I love it when your eyes are bright and mischievous like this."

She squints and looks up at me. "Did you use me as a fuck toy?" A smile teases the corner of her cheese-crumbed mouth.

"Maybe? I guess you'll only find out if you feel a drip." I can't hold back the laugh when her mouth opens into an "o".

"Caleb! You're back!" Steve's voice carries across the room as he strides in. Carmen's hurried steps keep her in pace with him.

"Steve! Man, great to see you! Crazy few months, huh?" Our palms collide in a fierce handshake before I pull him in for a tight hug.

He was a lean and lanky guy with disheveled hair when I last saw him, but he seems to have filled out a little. He's discovered a comb for his wild red locks as well.

The end of the world looks good on him.

"I heard you brought us something special." His blue eyes brighten as he extends his broad hand to Sarah. "What Carmen said you can do sounds pretty amazing. And you might just be the key that we've been missing. I'm Steve. I promise I won't turn you into a pin cushion."

"I'll vouch for him, baby." I slide next to her on the bench seat. "He's the only guy I've ever known that got fired because he wouldn't do unethical tests on mice." My arm wraps behind her waist.

I don't miss the grin on Steve's face as he catches me hugging her closer.

But, when he stands and stretches his own around Carmen's shoulders, I nearly choke on the piece of gouda I had pilfered off of the plate.

"Caleb? Are you okay?" Sarah's big green eyes pinch as she turns to smack me on the back.

After fighting a coughing fit, I nod and head towards the sink to grab some water.

Carmen follows me.

"I'm sure you're wondering...?" She starts, but lets the question fade.

"Not really. I'm happy for you. I thought you were too cold hearted to ever date." I grin around swallows from the cold glass.

"He saved my life. Twice. I know relationships at the workplace are against company policy." Her hands wring at her waist.

"Firstly, I quit, remember? Secondly, I don't give a shit who you're fucking if you can fix my wife."

I set the empty cup down on the counter before staring into Carmen's dark eyes. "Can you help her?"

Her lips aren't as full without the layers of makeup she always wore, but she spreads them in a broad smile. "Yes. I really think we can."

"Explain this again, please?" Sarah sits on the side of our bed and crosses her legs. Her waving toe matches the frustration exuding from her knotted arms and sour expression.

"It's simple. We have to get your viral load at the highest, and then put you under exertion so the inoculation has the fastest sweep possible through your body. If it works, we can pull your titers and it will help to formulate a more broad sweeping vaccine." I don't know how I can make it clearer.

"Caleb. What the hell is that? I'm a kindergarten teacher, not a scientist. Talk to me like I'm five for just this once." Her lower lip sticks out in a petulant pout.

My cock twitches watching her little flush of cranky work its way up her neck. "I need you hungry enough to phase out. Then I'm gonna make you sweat, baby." I drop my fists into the plush comforter on either side of her hips so I can take that teasing mouth between my teeth.

Her fingers wind into my hair as a giggle sneaks past her moan. "How are you gonna do that?" She darts the tiny pink triangle tip of her tongue out and licks the tip of my nose before she lays herself back onto the bed.

A growl works its way out of my chest as I flatten myself over her. "I'm going to make you my fuck-toy, like I promised." Penning her legs between my thighs, I let my hard-on push against her lower belly.

"You are?" Her sultry question turns into a shriek when I pin her hands above her head.

"Mmhm. The last thing you'll know is me being in you. Then, when you wake back up, all you'll feel is me. Loving you." I find the tender spot beneath her ear where I can feel her pulse race as I taste her.

Her sweet breath warms the hollow of my throat with her long sigh as her body wiggles beneath me.

"I like that idea. I'll be reborn on your dick. The second cumming." She erupts in full bellied laughter.

"Keep walking, baby. I know you're hungry. It won't be much longer." Sweat beads on her forehead as she dutifully marches on the treadmill I dragged into our room.

"My belly... is growling..." Her words are guttural.

I know she's struggling. It can't be easy losing control.

I just hope this works. The clinical trials went well in the models, but she's the first human to test it.

My beautiful guinea pig.

A pang coils in my gut. I've done this long enough to know that sometimes things don't go according to plan. The thought of something happening to her after everything we've been through nearly makes me sick to my stomach.

Her right foot starts to drag every few steps. The steady whine of the belt covers her low moan.

"Baby? Are you ready for me?" Dropping my boxers, I find a rhythmic step behind her on the machine.

"Yea." One syllable answers. She's almost gone.

"You're doing so good. Let me ease your pain. Spread those legs for me." I push the stop button as she obeys. Her movements are stilted, like it's a struggle for her body to listen.

Her arms stay stretched in front of her, tugging her supple back into taut silken lines for me to trace. Goosebumps follow the path of my finger's light tracing.

"This will be the last time you leave me. Then you're mine forever. Mind and body." Tasting the salty crook of her neck makes a pant tumble from her lips.

Fire races up my body as I press closer. My hands find their way down her smooth belly to the damp apex of her thighs.

My cock twitches thinking of how soon I can get her swollen with our baby. I want to feel her carrying new life. A birth of the best parts of us.

The proof of our survival would grow and thrive with us.

We both groan as I sink into her, but her's lengthens. Deepens. Morphs into a low growl.

She twists her body as her teeth snap inches from my arm. It's the tease of a snack that makes her shiver with desire.

Riding through this with her was my only choice. I know myself enough, I'd want her in my arms for this. Who knows what will happen. There is a zero percent chance that I would let this happen to her behind safety glass in a room full of people who don't know her.

Or love her as I do.

She's at her most dangerous and vulnerable. And, yet still harmless to me because I know I won't get infected.

The syringe sits on the shelf next to us. When I reach for it, it's as if she's drawn to it. She follows my movement, straining her clicking jaw to reach.

Every lure of my fingers has her tensing tighter and tighter around my cock. I'm almost tempted to let her take a bite as ferociously as her cunt is squeezing me.

It would be worth it. She can have my pinky if it means she clamps down on me hard enough to cut off the blood flow.

A stringer of drool slips from the edge of her mouth as her tongue pokes out in desperate longing for my flesh.

Yea, no. I think I'll keep my digits.

The number fourteen needle pierces the perfect globe of her ass cheek and I press the plunger on the viscous fluid to push it into her system.

Nausea rolls through me when the possible consequences begin to scroll through my thoughts, so I thrust myself into her to distract myself.

"Shouldn't take long, baby. Let me fuck you conscious." Grabbing her hips, I take long strokes as she thrashes against her tethers.

My balls ache and pressure builds in my limbs as her writhing billows the fire within me.

"Come on, Sarah. Find your way out." My thighs twitch with each thrust as I get closer to spilling over the edge.

I need her back. I don't want to fight this new world without her.

Her hair whips over my chest as her feverish skin sears me. She's burning from the inside. The sounds that she makes mirror the spike in her temperature.

Bending at the waist, her torso lays across the foam wrapped rails limply as her legs give out.

Only her rapid breathing lets me know she's still with me.

Holding her lower body, I slow my pace until we're both still.

Waiting is the hardest part.

"Please, baby? Fight. I know you can do it." I don't want to let her go. My lips trail soft kisses along her spine, scorching my lips with each touch.

A low groan whispers from her. She flexes a shaky leg before putting some of her weight on it.

"That's it. You got this." Letting myself withdraw almost all of the way out of her tight pussy, I slam back into her.

She grunts.

Well, I might have to try that again.

Two more hard thrusts earns me a longer groan, punctuated by the slapping of our thighs.

It's like I'm trying to start a reluctant motor with my dick.

The faster I move, the longer and louder the sounds that come out of her.

"Fuck, baby. I'm so close." Grabbing her shoulder gives me better leverage.

She continues the motion, grinding into me before she tilts her head back.

"I love you, Caleb," she screams as her body clenches onto me in a suffocating climax.

Hearing her voice tears away the last thread of restraint. I've never orgasmed this hard in my life. Every muscle in my body spasms as ribbons of cum erupt from the depths of me.

Ecstasy and relief surges through me.

She came back to me, without a bite to eat. The terror and fear that has hidden in the shadows around me for weeks disappears.

I want to spin her around and shout in victory to the world.

"I love you, too. Welcome back, baby." The velcro straps rip away as my spent cock slides out of her.

She turns and throws her arms around my neck, peppering my face with frantic kisses.

"I can't believe it. It really happened." Tears stream her cheeks and her fingers bury into my beard, pulling me to her to press her mouth fervently to mine.

Sarah hasn't had a remission. It worked.

But, finding a cure for the general population has hit a hiccup.

"We can't find enough." Carmen's crossed arms stick out from her chest as she stares at the whiteboard. "There has to be more. We have broad spectrum radio transmissions, flyers being dropped, and relief teams spreading the word. Any other ideas?"

"Can we synthesize it?" I jot down more ideas even as I ask the top one on my list.

The original staff numbered in the hundreds. There's less than twenty of us here.

What we lack in numbers, we make up for in determination.

After Sarah's recovery, we were able to pull enough antibodies from her blood to easily cure the world in just a few vials.

It's the other crucial ingredient we're missing. Our fluke patient in Vegas was like hitting the lottery. An aberration in the virus gave one woman exceptional healing rates.

"No. We've tried replicating the enzyme found in those stem cells, but no matter what we've tried, they fail. Only using the original cord blood were we able to make the first, and only, batch of one hundred doses." Carmen's hand works over the board, filling in numbers and requirements.

Survivors are out there. Chances are, there's more with that miraculous mutation like the mother and father of that baby have. And millions of infected that are still early enough in their illness to be cured.

But, to cure them all, it's daunting.

"We will likely be able to streamline the system to be able to get as many as a thousand viable doses from a single source." She turns to face the group with thinly pressed lips. "It will be a losing battle waiting for her to have another baby, if she chooses to. And the new dad would have to have the factor. Her husband, who had it, died early in the initial chaos."

"Can't we just make her?" A man's voice calls from the back of the room.

Tony. Of course it is.

"And, what, exactly, are you proposing?" Carmen's eyes narrow as she glares at him. "Strap her down to a bed and rape her? Are you volunteering? We are still civilized. Just because we have an unlimited budget provided by the remains of our government, doesn't mean we should turn into savages." She throws her hands in the air, her voice raises with each word. "Her husband had the healing factor, too. They both did. Do you? Without that pair up, it's a waste of time."

She turns back to the board. "Asshole."

Steve and I are the only ones close enough to hear her mutter the word. We share a grin over her irritation.

Keep eye on Tony goes in my notes.

Now that he's voiced it, I lose what little trust I had in him.

Funny how some people have used this apocalypse to turn into animals. The stories come in every day of the atrocities that are happening.

There just aren't enough military and police left to deal with any of it. Armies and city states have formed, all with their own rules.

If we can't get a cure going out wide, quickly, civilization as we know it will greatly change.

"We need more ways to reach the right people. There has to be more out there like her." Carmen pops the top on her marker and starts adding more things to her own list as ideas get shouted from the room.

"Excuse me, ma'am?" A blonde haired woman steps into the conference room with a piece of paper squeezed into her fist.

I think she's one of the tech's wives. Everyone's family has moved into the research facility. It's safe, and we get regular helicopter supply drops. The global population is counting on us.

"Yes, Eva." Carmen holds out her hand for the crumpled note.

The blushing woman drops it quickly and dashes out the door.

Carmen's dark eyes widen before she steps over to where Steve and I sit and she slides the message in front of us. "There might be hope after all."

"What does this say? In exchange for what?" Steve squints as he tries to read it before handing it to me.

I can read even less.

But, one thing stands out in scrawled letters.

Confirmed match

It looks like it's from one of our guys working in the Los Angeles area.

Holy shit. A needle in a haystack.

Chapter 21

Peter

"Only the asshole, Sully. I told you that! Get out of her pussy, it's mine." I shove into her with both of my hard cocks, breaking through the membrane of her virginity like it's the first time.

Fuck it never stops feeling good.

Sully pulls back and lets a stringer of spit fall in a slow line to the tip of his dick.

"Don't waste your time, she likes it rough." To emphasize my point, I lean over and bite down on her nipple hard enough to draw the metallic taste of blood into my mouth.

She whimpers and tugs at the chains binding her wrists.

"Like that, my queen bee? Or do you like big ol' Johnny's pecker better?" I glance across to check and make sure the dumb shit is in the right hole.

He's so fucking stupid, he'd confuse his own dick with a sausage if they got too close together on a table.

The big man stutters through his clenched teeth as his face gets red. With a loud groan, he spasms and collapses across her, his fat face almost touching my belly.

"Get the hell away from me, Johnny. I don't want you next to my dicks." Stinging a slap over the rolls on his neck makes him cuss under his breath and move away.

"I didn't want to hurt her belly, boss. This one's getting big." Johnny pushes himself up, his massive softening cock slipping out from her. The mixture of blood, shit, and cum makes it stick to his thigh as he stands back. "Nasty. Where's the towels?" His massive frame shuffles away to the bathroom with his pants still hugging his knees.

That's my baby bump. The thought of so many of my kids running around with the god-like healing power makes my balls tighten and I pump a double load of my hot seed into her fresh pussy.

I think I can make at least one more.

When I walked out that cold morning five months ago, it took me days to get past the surprise of seeing her strapped down to the merry go round with two full lower torsos. Split in the middle where my knife had fileted her, she grew a completely new set of legs out of each wound.

I figured out how to do it again.

Like a fucking starfish, pussy galore at each split.

Tucking my duo-dicks back into my jeans, I smack Sully hard enough on his bare ass cheek he loses his own nut deep in her asshole.

I'm going to have to start numbering her slots to keep track of them.

Just before I step out of the room, the bitch calls after me. "Peter, if you're done I need untied. I need to eat. Send

Missy in with some stew and to help me." She rattles her restraints and has the audacity to huff at me.

"New helper this week." I had to send Missy back into the ward. She fought me too hard when I pinned her in the walk in cooler and made her suck me off. Now, she's collared to the bottom of the stairs trying to eat her own arm off after I made sure she got infected.

There are consequences to saying "no" to me.

Jeremy's young daughter sits on the bench outside the door with her hands clasped tightly on her lap.

The look of fear in her eyes when she looks up at me makes my left cock twitch.

"Why are you here?" I growl at her.

Her thin arm pops up clutching a piece of paper. As soon as my fingers close around it she darts down the hall.

Guess she's smarter than her dad.

Helicopter due in with first payment
Sending small team to do blood tests

Looks like we'll have some visitors today bearing gifts.

When I get to the bottom of the stairs, I nearly trip over Missy's splayed legs. The noise she's making has me glancing over at her naked form.

Both of her hands are digging at her crotch before she pulls up her fingers coated in blood to her mouth. Her manic tongue works its way between every crevice as she licks the bright red from her hand.

I wonder if she's on the rag, or eating herself from the pussy out.

No, actually I don't give a shit. She gave terrible head.

The cook jumps when I push through the swinging door into the kitchen.

"Can I help you, boss?" His thin hands fold in front of him in a small bow showing the bald spot on the top of his head.

"Nah, just letting you know that the little cream pie tied to the stairs will be ready soon. Another big batch of stew for all of our citizens." She doesn't have a lot of meat on her, but she'll feed everyone in the soup line for another couple of days.

His mustache twitches and his cheeks pale. "Very good, sir. I'll get Jeremy to help me."

"Tell him his daughter is getting old enough to start earning her keep around here." I saw those hips on her. She's starting to get some curves.

He doesn't reply, just gives me a short nod before it looks like he's going to puke in the sink.

Whatever. If he fucks up, he can go in the pot next.

There's no way I'm sharing my food with the rest of the freeloaders. The helpful ones are working on growing their own. Some have even brought some livestock like chickens and shit. Sully does a good job at leading the scavenging teams.

Anyone who doesn't pull their share, ends up feeding the camp anyways.

It's a beautiful system.

The thump of the helicopter reverberates through the mansion, drawing me past Missy to go outside.

It lands in the middle of the main lawn and two lanky men climb out.

I think I'll wait here at the top of the steps for them to come to me. One has a dark beard and walks just a little ahead of the other.

"Caleb." His broad hand goes out for a handshake.

"Peter."

"Steve." The red head has a firm grip, too.

Both of them have the thousand yard look in their eyes like they've seen some shit.

"The blood testing won't take long. Here's the payment as agreed." Caleb holds out a silver briefcase which I barely keep from snatching out of his hand.

"Cheek swabs. Blood tests. What's next? Do I come in a cup?" I flash him a grin before unlocking the case.

Well fuck me sideways. Two kilos of medical grade coke and a big bag of oxy. At least, that's what the little tags say. *Property of the United States Government*

I always knew they had the good shit.

Sully hasn't been able to find anything worth a damn for weeks. One of the downsides of my new ability is drugs and booze just don't hit the way they used to.

But, with this, I'll be able to get wasted.

Leading them into the building, I set the payment on the table where Sully sits. "We got the first drop, man. Just for knocking up the bitch." I push it across to him. "Test it. Make sure it's for real."

Waving my hand at the two guys, they follow me past Missy still eating her own cunt paste as we go upstairs.

"Jesus." Steve makes a gagging sound when we reach her room and step in.

"What the—" Caleb turns away with the back of his wrist shoved against his mouth.

"You're pussies. She's the perfect queen bee. Aren't you, baby?" I step around the bed and make a show of putting a kiss on her forehead.

Jessica nods from where she's propped up on pillows with a big ceramic bowl of stew. Her new helper, Jane, sits off to the side with big doe eyes watching me.

That one might stick around for a while. She's too damned ugly for me.

"How in the fuck?" Caleb steps back into the room, his eyes riveted to her naked lower body.

All four pairs of her legs are folded primly at the ankles.

My girl is a proper priss.

"Caleb?" She leans forward and pulls a sheet over her legs. "What the fuck are you doing here? You better not have brought Levi!" Her voice raises until it hurts my ears.

"No, Jess. I didn't. He died that night." The tall man's jaw tightens and his brow drops as he glares at her.

"Well. I see you're old friends. Let's get this over with before I have to kill you for making my queen mad." I fold my arms over my chest.

She might be a bitch, but she's mine.

The red headed guy steps up and pulls out a small kit with a needle and vials.

Jessica covers her arms under the blanket. "No. You can't have any of my blood. I'm not helping you."

My hand finds the back of her neck. Squeezing hard enough to get her attention, I turn her head to face me. "Do as he says, and I'll do that thing for you."

The amber in her eyes grows until her pupils almost disappear. "Okay."

Her thin elbow appears and opens for the Steve guy to get what he needs.

"Jess...how did this happen?" Caleb asks in a hushed tone.

My chest puffs out. "I did it." And damn proud of it. She's giving me a never ending supply of virgin pussy because of it. Her shit grows back every night so I get to rip her apart every morning.

Heaven.

Caleb shakes his head and stares at her form hidden beneath the thin fabric. "Unbelievable." His words are barely a whisper.

"See? I always told everyone I was special. Now, you can see it." She flips her golden hair behind her shoulder. "I'm better than everyone." Her snub nose turns up in the air and her eyes flick over me in disdain.

I catch her jab. She'll pay for that one.

"Her first one is due in about three months. If you want the baby shit, or whatever, you better have someone here. *With* my stuff. No snuff, no access." I want to lay down the rules now.

Steve puts the full vial in his little kit and motions for me to offer my arm. "We'll hold up our end of the deal." He doesn't look up as he pokes into one of my protruding veins.

No pain I've ever endured will compare to having my dick cut in half.

He's done before I notice, and the two of them hustle out the door.

Jessica turns her face up to me, hope sparkling in her eyes. "So? Do I get my parade?"

"Do you really think you deserve having the entire camp tell you how beautiful and amazing you are, after you throw me under the bus like that? You're my wife. And you made me sound like trash. That gets punished."

Her fingers claw at me as I walk away. "No! Please! No! I'm sorry!"

It only takes me a moment to find what I'm looking for in the huge garage. Still sitting where I left it after last time.

Just needs a fresh battery.

Terror flashes across her face when I re-enter her room.

I pull the trigger on the sawzall for effect, so she can watch the blade rapidly cut the air.

Like it's going to do to her.

"No! Fuck! I'm sorry! You're the best! Better than me!" Her palms wave at me to stop, but she can't run.

"I was just thinking this morning how I needed another fresh pussy to fuck. Since you have babies in those two, I want a new one." Tearing the sheet from her leaves her body exposed. All eight legs bend and kick out at me in defense.

It's a struggle working my way between her flailing limbs, but I manage to sink the long blade with its deep wood cutting teeth into her cunt causing a squirt of blood to pour out.

Jane sits trembling in the chair nearby, her knuckles white as she grips the arms.

"We're gonna give those people something to see at your next parade." Her struggles are making me so hard, I jerk my zipper down, freeing my hard cocks. Gripping her thigh, I spread her next set of legs wide enough to shove my hips closer.

Stabbing her with my dicks, I feed one into her clenching pussy, and the other into her tight little asshole before turning on the saw.

Chapter 22

Sarah

His tiny red face searches open mouthed until I maneuver my nipple between his little lips. With ferocious zeal, he guzzles down his first taste.

"He's like you, cranky when he's hungry." Caleb's lips press against my temple with a teasing grin.

I'm too tired to laugh, but he's not wrong. Hunger doesn't drive my mind away, but I still get awfully motivated to find food when it's time. "With his long arms and legs, I have a feeling it's going to take a lot to keep him satisfied."

Caleb slides onto the bed to sit next to me, propping himself on his arm framing my hips. His dark eyes are filled with love as he watches me.

I have everything I could ever want, right here.

We're safe and taken care of, in a world that is slowly recovering from the devastating plague.

My finger traces the head of my newborn on my breast. His soft skin, the fine strands of his dark hair, the round cheeks drooping as he falls gently asleep.

He's perfect.

A tear slips from my eye and leaves a droplet on his miniature clenched fingers. He startles enough to look up at me with his baby blues, the spitting image of his name sake.

Levi.

"I'm so damned proud of you. Let's have thirty more." Caleb's teeth flash in a broad grin as he rolls off the bed

"I'm game. Just give me a few days." I want a million of them.

There's only four kids here at the facility, but I've been able to start helping give regular classes. It's been a great challenge learning how to teach the variety in ages at once.

I can't wait until the room is bursting with youth and vigor. So many people have died in the last year, it's almost overwhelming to think about.

Caleb won't tell me much about the new donors that are providing the essential cord blood for the cure. He said it's one of the few things that need to stay classified for his job.

The horror on his face when he returns after every gathering trip tells me I probably don't want to know.

He did say it is motivation for them to find a way to synthesize the protein.

There's discussion of setting up re-training camps for those that are cured. Some don't come back with all of their faculties. The virus caused a lot of damage to their brains, but at least they're alive and not completely mindless.

Hope carries us forward. It's ironic that something designed to offer help and comfort turned out to be the most horrific travesty humanity has encountered in eight hundred years.

Not since the time of the black plague have such a high percentage of people died.

We have a cure, though. The only struggle is getting it to enough people.

Let's just hope it doesn't mutate.

M.A. Cobb

AUTHOR

Trapped beneath the city of Seattle when an irreversible darkness falls, Carly and James discover more than just light at the end of the tunnel. As they flee the impending collapse of society, chaos and danger are around every turn. Finally escaping the confines of the suffocating streets, they find that their temporary sanctuary in a small town has its own set of perils. Will their love survive the threat in the shadows that pursue them?

https://mybook.to/WZvfY

Coming soon:

Burst of Retribution

A year after the world goes black, Maddy decides to leave the safety of her new home to check on the family she left behind. But when she finds her childhood home empty, she discovers that the darkness in her past is merely the beginning of something more dire. Struggling to fight the memories, she's forced to choose to rescue her family, or fall victim to the darkness again. Captured by a man whose intentions are unknown, will she be able to escape to find the justice she deserves?

The Dire Reaction

As a veterinarian, Dr. Danielle Michelson was excited to be involved with a new genetic therapy designed to help fight a common pet
ailment. She even knew the perfect canine to enroll in the treatment, one belonging to the tall blond cowboy, Sam Downing.
Little did she know, while things were heating up between them, the world itself was transforming.
The cure turned into a curse, and created an army of monsters that thrive on pure chaos and destruction. The worst of them all, was someone they
both knew.

Now, they must find allies to fight back against the onslaught of carnal evil that threatens to overtake them.

Will Dani and Sam survive the monstrous terror that is overrunning their city? Or will the hordes of ravenous creatures consume everything, and
everyone, in their path?

https://mybook.to/FoQnj

The Dire Legacy

After the virus ravaged the earth, it left a wake of men and terrifying monsters, vying for power.

But, sometimes, the monsters were not the ones with fur. Sometimes, they look like you and I.

Michael
fled the only home he knew before his truth was revealed. Was he a
monster like his father? Or did the world around him change so much he
no longer fit in?

When he meets Hope, everything he
thought he knew shifts. She redefines this new world, and reveals the
true evil that still walks among us.

https://mybook.to/czgbgIe

Curse of the Mourning Ring

Alice, a reclusive author, has spent her life hiding behind her computer and only writing about love. But her hopes soon falter as she stumbles upon a little wooden box beneath the twisted roots of a fallen oak tree. Inside she finds a long forgotten heirloom.

A ring bound to a fierce man who had died a hundred years ago.

A ring that pulls his dark, tortured soul to her.

She can hear him.

She can feel him.

But can she love him?

Henry's life ended in betrayal. An oath he swears upon his father's ring holds him back from eternal peace, tethering his spirit to this plane.

He moves amongst the living, unseen and intangible.

A man out of time, out of touch.

There is only one thing in his grasp.

There is only her. She is his everything.

Will he win her love, or is he destined to linger in her shadow eternally?

https://mybook.to/W9Vgv

Nikolai Petrov: The Petrov Family

Nikolai lost his wife nearly a decade ago in a brutal act of
retaliation from a rival family. His years of solitude were spent
bathing in the blood of revenge until a tentative peace was made.

It's only after the daughter of his best friend sneaks into his
life that he learns how thin that cease-fire really is.

She may be what he needs to heal, but will it be at the cost of his empire?

https://mybook.to/KGePAM